BUTTERWORTH
TAKES A
VACATION

CHAPTER ONE

It was the second coming of Christ. I bolted up in bed, breathing hard. As another shrill ring pierced the darkness, my arms flailed in the direction of lamps, books, clock radios, and tissue boxes on my nightstand.

Finally, I grabbed for a phone. "Hello?" I mumbled into the base of a lamp.

The ringing persisted. After saying "Hello" into a John Grisham novel, a Kleenex box, and the Bible, I finally found the antenna connected to the cordless phone on my nightstand.

"Hello?" I gasped.

"Bill? It's your ol' buddy Edmund. How ya doin', big guy?"

"Edmund? What time is it?"

"It's 2:34 a.m." Edmund Holmes, being a certified public accountant, would never think of answering, "Around 2:35" or worse yet, "Um, 2:30-ish." He often tacks on "Pacific Daylight Time."

"What on earth is wrong?" I asked. "Is Jenny okay? Any problem with the girls?"

"No problems at all, buddy." As Edmund laughed, more of my brain clicked in, and I began to get the picture. Edmund had another of his "ideas" that he couldn't wait to share with me.

Edmund is a night person. I am not. Of course, I'm not a day person, either. I have a couple of good hours around lunch, that's about it. Yet somehow, Edmund and I have forged a friendship that has withstood potentially divisive issues like the fact that he makes a lot more money and flaunts it by driving the car of my dreams, a black Lexus ES 300.

"Edmund?"

"Yes?"

"Why are you calling me in the middle of the night? It's really late. Is this perhaps something that can wait till morning?"

"Whoa Nellie! No way! Jenny and I were just sitting in bed here having the greatest conversation."

"Go on," I prodded, hoping to get to the point.

"Well, we think we've come up with a wonderful idea!"

This was getting ludicrous. The honest truth was that all I wanted was to get back to my soft, comforting, *waiting* pillow. No idea could be worth waking a person for. Even sitting there in the dark, I could picture Edmund's long, thin face, bursting with enthusiasm all the way from his receding hairline to his cleft chin.

"Okay, here goes," he said. "Tom and Meg Graham have been taking vacations with us the last couple of years. Well, this year we've decided to take a week and camp out down on the central California coast. Between the Grahams' Winnebagel and our tent trailer, we've got tons of room." (Edmund often mispronounces certain words. It's not a geographic thing like "warsh" or "pak the cahh," it's something to do with how he sees, or fails to see, the world.)

"So," he continued, "since it'll just be Tom and Meg and Jenny and me with our two girls, we thought it would be fantastic if Bill and all the Butterworth kids came along with us on the camping trip! Isn't that a super idea?"

"Bill?

"Bill?

"Bill, are you asleep?"

I wished I was. Ah, sleep, the ultimate Christian escape...the believer's equivalent to drugs, model airplane glue, or double martinis.

How could I tell my best friend that I have absolutely, positively no interest whatsoever in anything that even closely resembles the horrors of *camping* ?

"Bill? Are you still there?"

"Yes. I'm here, Edmund."

"I guess it is such an amazing offer that it kinda takes your breath away!"

I could hear Edmund passing on my "ecstatic reaction" to Jenny. Her excited giggle signaled to me that I was in deep grease here.

"Edmund, can I have a little time to think this over? It's a big decision and I should probably talk to the kids about it." By now I had wadded up all the bedsheets into a giant ball.

I was definitely stressing.

"No problem-o!" Edmund answered. "Take your good ol' time. Pass on all the good news to your kiddos and I'll give you a jingle at work some time tomorrow morning, okay?"

"Edmund," I answered, an edge to my voice, "This *is* tomorrow morning."

As we hung up, I was overcome with the idea that I should have stuck with my first impulse when the phone rang—and conversed with the base of the lamp.

Morning came in a few short hours. At five-thirty the air in the Sierra foothills was cool, crisp, and clean. Most folks who lived in our little town of Pine Woods had been commenting on how we missed out on spring this year. We went from the cold, rainy days of winter right into the very hot days of summer.

This was especially hard on the students and their teachers, like me. When it feels like summer, it doesn't feel like school. I was thrilled that we were in our last few days of classes over at Pine Woods Community College where I teach.

I jumped out of bed with nursing home speed, throwing on my trusty green robe. This robe has served me well over the years, ever since I brought it home after finding it hanging in the closet at a fancy hotel in Boston. The colors reminded me of the Celtics and wearing it made me feel like Larry Bird.

I shuffled to the kitchen for the morning ritual of packing five brown-bag lunches—one for each of the boys and one for me. This is a routine I could perform blindfolded.

Next, I turned my attention to the coffeepot that had, thanks to its automatic timer, produced the nectar of life for another groggy morning. I love coffee, anytime, anywhere. I like to think of myself as a coffee connoisseur, a purist in the world of the black bean. But I am treated with some ambivalence by other coffee fanatics because I am a firm believer in the use of cream and sugar.

Meanwhile, my four sons descended into the kitchen. All five of my kids, including my daughter Betsy, have their dad's white hair and blue eyes, as well as my inability to tan.

The boys began ransacking the pantry for any sort of cereal that's not necessarily good for you.

I try not to buy those sugary cereals that rot teeth, but somehow there is always a box to be found. The boys carefully hide it behind my box of natural bran. They know with certainty I will only use that box when it is well with my soul, but not with my middle-aged digestive system.

BJ is eighteen, Brandon is sixteen, Ben is fourteen, and Bo is ten. Each seated himself at the dining room table with his own personal box of cereal.

"Dad, what was going on in your bedroom last night around 2:30?" Brandon asked. "It sounded like things were crashing on the floor! Did you have some sort of nightmare?"

"The phone rang!" Bo answered on my behalf, his face exploding into a huge smile. "Daddy always knocks everything off his nightstand before he finds the phone!"

Four children laughed.

"Who called at that hour?" Ben asked. I was about to answer, but BJ interrupted.

"Must've been Edmund," he said. "He's the only person I know that would do something like that."

"What is it this time?" Brandon piped in. "Was he trimming his backyard at 2:00 in the morning, so he called to see if he could borrow your weed-whacker?"

Now I was laughing, too.

"Maybe he couldn't sleep," added Bo, my ten-year-old. He immediately cracked up, but he was the only one at the table who thought this was a humorous observation. It's difficult being ten, the youngest, and working a tough crowd like this one.

"Actually, Edmund called to invite all of us to go with his family and the Grahams on a camping trip along the coast this summer!" I doubled over in uncontrollable hysterics. It took me a while to realize I'd made a big tactical error, and like Bo had, laughed alone.

"That sounds like a great idea, Dad!" Ben began.

"It sure does," added Bo and Brandon.

"Sweet deal, Pops," BJ concurred.

"We haven't been camping in a long time," Ben mused as he scratched his chin. The others nodded in agreement.

"Don't you realize *why* it has been such a long time since we've been camping?" My face was slowly turning red and my neck veins were starting to do the conga.

As if on cue, all four boys shrugged their shoulders.

"Well, *I* know why it's been so long since we've been camping—because I tend to recall moments of terror more readily than any of you do!"

Suddenly the cereal bowls in front of each son became absolutely mesmerizing. They dropped their heads and stared bullets into their bowls.

Right then, nineteen-year-old Betsy, who was home from college, emerged from her room. "So much for sleeping in," she lamented. "But I thought it would be the boys who would wake me up, not *you*, Dad."

Betsy's long blonde hair was disheveled, but nothing could diminish her good looks, especially in her dad's eyes.

"I'm sorry to wake you, sweetie," I apologized as I kissed her forehead, "but we're having a little disagreement out here, and I guess I got a tad carried away."

"What are we arguing about?" she asked.

"We've been invited on a camping trip!" Bo volunteered.

"Cool!" Betsy cooed.

"No, not cool," I countered.

"Are you kidding, Dad?" she asked sincerely.

"Listen to me, gang. I'm serious about this." I was starting to feel like a male Wicked Witch of the Sierra. "The last time we went camping was a disaster. Do you remember what happened during the last camp out?" I shouted.

All five kids just dropped their heads in silent rebuke.

"It was a long time ago...even before Bo and Benjamin were born."

Betsy, BJ, and Brandon nodded slowly, not sure if they wanted to go on record as recalling the disaster.

"Some things are better forgotten and never repeated," I said. "So don't be getting your minds set on some sort of group visit to Smokey the Bear, because it's just not gonna happen."

"Aww, rats," came a whispered voice from Ben.

"Whatever," was Brandon's cool reply.

"Fine," Betsy spoke softly.

"I'll try to understand," said BJ, the mature voice of reason.

"I don't have much more time with BJ," I mused. "Just like Betsy left last year, he'll be leaving soon, too. This summer might be my last real significant time with—" I stopped myself. Their eyes betrayed the polite answers they gave seconds ago.

You've got to stay tough, I told myself. *Hey, your parents never did things they absolutely didn't want to do just because you did. Kids toed the line back then. Kids knew their place. No spoiled brats, no miniature leaders running the show, and no wimpy parents! Yeah, Butterworth, be strong and hold your ground!*

But then Bo lifted his head and I saw his big blue eyes filled with tears, and I almost started crying myself.

Now you know how I ended up taking a camping vacation.

✛

True to his word, Edmund called later that morning to check in with me. "So, how did the kids respond to your great news?" he gushed with genuine enthusiasm.

"They were thrilled, Edmund," I replied.

"Well I'm not surprised," my friend reflected. "It has the makings of one fine vacation!"

"I can't wait."

"By the way," Edmund continued, "Tom Graham and I are meeting down at the Pine Woods Hardware Store to discuss the trip, so why don't you join us?"

"Oh, I don't know..." I stammered. Shooting the breeze about Coleman stoves, state-of-the-art hatchets, and the pros and cons of certain types of tent pegs offered no appeal to this city boy.

"Come on, Bill, we need your input," he insisted.

"When it comes to camping, Edmund, *I have no input*," I stressed.

"Whoa Nellie!" Edmund wheezed in between large belly laughs that I could hear from my end of the phone. "Don't be so modest, Bill. I know for a fact that you've been camping before! It was several years ago, right?"

I took a deep breath, swallowed hard, and spoke as calmly as I could: "Look, Edmund, I might as well tell you up front. I feel ambivalent about this trip. Part of me doesn't want to go, and the other part of me *really* doesn't want to go!"

"Did something happen during your last camp out?" Edmund, CPA and master of the obvious, inquired.

"Let's just say it involved a large animal, a zipper that was stuck, and a search and rescue team."

"Wow!" said Edmund.

"So just don't be so pushy," I snapped back. "You CPAs are all alike. You think if you get all the facts, you just crank out some numbers that will make everything work out nicely. Well, life isn't that simple, Edmund, so *deal with it!*"

"Okay," Edmund replied softly.

"Look, I don't want to talk about it anymore...maybe some other time. I've got to go now, anyway. What time are you and Tom getting together?"

"At 12:30."

"Okay. I'll see what I can do. Maybe I can join you for at least a little bit of this hike through Hardware Heaven."

"That would be great, Bill," Edmund replied.

As I hung up the phone, I felt my stomach tighten and I unconsciously opened my top right-hand desk drawer, pulling out a jumbo jar of Tums. I poured a half dozen fruit-flavored little tablets out of the bottle and popped them in my mouth.

I started pacing in my tiny office, which is really more like a medium-size closet or shed. I teach in the communications department. Students hate taking speech class, the college hates unhappy students, therefore I am in an office that resembles a walk-in pantry.

After a few hours of paperwork interspersed with worry and despair, I glanced at my wristwatch to discover it was almost time to meet Edmund and Tom. What was I getting into?

I had never been camping as a child. I was born and raised in the city of Philadelphia, not Yellowstone Park. Camping was an oddity that some of my friends participated in while growing up, but not our family.

Once or twice in my childhood we embarked on what is considered a major vacation for a northeasterner. I'm referring to the trip south to Florida. We'd drive all day and then pick out a motel that had the two biggest drawing cards a kid could ask for: *a swimming pool* and *a color television*.

The only time I'd camped as an adult was the time I didn't want to tell Edmund about. I had gone with several other fathers and their kids. No trailers or extras. Just pup tents. I didn't know what to do and so I hung around with this one dad because he seemed to know what he was doing, and he was the biggest guy in the group. I figured he could protect me in case of any danger in the middle of the night.

We set up camp, we ate the raw food we tried to cook over the fire, we did the campfire singing thing, we even told ghost stories, which was a really big mistake. By bedtime, everyone was scared out of his mind. I had my three kids in the tent with me, along with my large friend, Fred, and his two boys.

I made a big mistake when I chose Fred to share a tent with. The fact that he was the largest guy on the trip only guaranteed that he was the biggest fraidy-cat in our group.

About two in the morning Fred asked me if I heard something, and unfortunately, I did. And it just had to be a bear. That big old thing came right up to our tent and we could hear him batting at the side of it with one of his huge paws.

I was frightened, but Fred was ballistic. He started screaming at the top of his lungs, "We're all gonna die!" He grabbed his two boys, clutching them to his chest, singing "Nearer My God to Thee" at the top of his voice. Of course, by now all the kids were awake and crying, thanks to Fred's brave and rational response.

There was a bear outside our tent and the brave one in our group was *me!*

Eventually the bear left. He was probably deafened by a grown man's screams. Once we thought the coast was clear, we all wanted out of the tent to get some air. But the zipper on the tent was stuck—in the zipped position. Fred pointed out how lucky we were that it was stuck closed, not open. "That bear would've had us for a midnight buffet," he said with feeling.

Then, Fred freaked out. "I'm claustrophobic!" he bellowed. One of the other guys camping in another tent finally called 911 on his cell phone, and they sent out a search-and-rescue team. They cut us out of the tent with one of those big, jagged-edged hunting knives—the "jaws of life" for the tent-enclosed. I could swear that the rescue guys were laughing the whole time.

I made a vow to God that night: no more camping for me or my family, ever....

✦

It was a beautiful afternoon. The sun shone brightly through the tall pine trees that surround our little hamlet. It was hot, but bearable. The nice weather, coupled with the thought that Tom Graham would also be with Edmund, brought a note of calm to my tumultuous lower intestinal track.

Tom is somewhat of a hero to me. Tall, tan, and together, that's Tom. He's a successful businessman, with an adoring, attractive wife, well-behaved kids, and two benchmark attributes: he loves the Lord and he used to play for the Dodgers. Perhaps Tom could put this camp-out into perspective.

Edmund showed up in his CPA uniform: blue button-down oxford dress shirt with red striped necktie and penny loafers—standard issue for the world of the accountant. Apparently anything less conservative would distract them from their bean-counting duties.

Tom, an entrepreneur working out of his home, wore a powder-blue golf shirt with a pair of khaki shorts, sweat socks, and Nikes. The whole outfit highlighted his excellent tan. I, on the other hand, had made a vow with God *never* to wear shorts without the express written consent of those who will view the two lily-white appendages known on other humans as legs.

I should probably confess at this juncture that I suffer from a rare malady. It's called Clothes/Laundry Obsessive Disorder, or CLOD for short. I am fascinated by the clothes that people wear and tend to memorize their entire outfits from day to day. Also, at home, I instinctively memorize the contents of the laundry hampers that fill our place. It's a seldom-discovered chemical imbalance. It's so rare that at one point the medical community referred to it as Butterworth's Syndrome; then we came up with CLOD.

At the Pine Woods Hardware Store Tom gave me a bear hug like we had fought in 'Nam together. "How is everything in the Graham household?" I asked, breaking free from his grasp.

"We're doing outstanding!" he replied. Tom was always super-positive, but he could get away with it.

"Tom's getting his Winnebagel all checked out so it'll be in tip-top condition for the trip!" Edmund added, jumping aboard the emotional Camping Choo Choo.

Edmund's excitement heightened my fears. "Guys, I don't know about this whole idea," I confessed.

"Whatever do you mean, buddy?" Tom sounded concerned.

"It's just that I'm not into camping like you two are. I think of myself as more highly evolved. Sleeping on the ground and cooking your own grub has all the appeal of diaper duty in the infants' Sunday school class."

"Now, now, I won't hear any more of this kind of talking," Tom chided. "Camping is an activity that brings families together... even Gary Smalley says so! I think you may have some bad past experiences that are shading your outlook."

Edmund was nodding his agreement. I was clearly outnumbered.

"You owe it to your kids," Edmund added. "You can't spend every vacation cooped up in a stuffy hotel room. You've got to experience the Great Outdoors!"

I was just about to debate with Edmund the validity of the phrase "cooped up in a stuffy hotel room" when Tom jumped in.

"So what do you think, buddy?"

"I guess I'm outvoted," I said, remembering Bo's eyes. "When do we leave?" I tried to laugh, but it hurt.

"That's the spirit!" Tom cheered. "Bill, that reminds me. Do you like to fish?"

"Eat fish?"

"No, *catch* fish."

"Yes, I love to eat fish."

"Do you go fishing a lot?"

"Only at certain restaurants…and never in Omaha." I felt like throwing up, and I wondered briefly about my own masculinity.

To me, the only thing worse than a camping trip was the idea of smelly old worms hanging murderously off a hook in an effort to dupe and kill another of God's creations. Maybe we could pack a pistol and murder land-roving animals as well. Maybe we could print up T-shirts for "The 1997 Blood and Guts Tour."

Then again, who knew? Maybe it would be fun.

Chapter Two

We went to church Sunday as always. I had a specific reason, however, on this particular Lord's Day. I went to earnestly pray that God would smile down on us during this upcoming adventure. And pray I did. My kids had to shake me back to consciousness when the sermon began.

While the pastor elaborated on the merits of good parenting, I silently prayed, "Dear Lord, please don't let anything bad happen on this trip. You know I think of camping much like a prostate exam, so I am providing you with a most excellent opportunity to teach me something new. Show me the error of my ways by allowing this camping trip to be like a day at the circus, or room service at the Maui Marriott, or a trip to Disneyland (where I'd much rather be going, but I digress, Lord).

"Of course, if you want to intercede, causing the whole trip to be canceled, you'll have no gripe from this child of God."

Inspired, I pushed on, "Lord, it's okay with me if you allow me to look totally macho as Camper Man on this trip. I want to be a real camper dude. Let the campfire go out on Tom, not me. Let it be Edmund's tent trailer that leaks buckets, not mine. Let me wield a mighty axe as Edmund suffers from heat exhaustion, as well as any number of gastrointestinal disorders. And please, Lord, keep me away from all the lions, tigers, and bears. You remember my last camping trip—when I vowed to never go anywhere in a tent again!"

Here I was briefly interrupted while Betsy nudged me and whispered, "Dad, are you asleep? Dad? I think you might be embarrassing me."

"I'm just praying, sweetheart," I said. "But I can do that with my eyes open."

"I want to remind you, Lord," I continued, fixing my eyes on a slightly purple hairdo in front of me, "that I have lousy medical insurance. If something happens to one of the kids out at the campsite, not only would it hurt him or her, but it could bury me financially. I don't want Edmund to take a spin in Tom's Winnebago only to run over one of my boys. So please keep us safe, dear Lord.

"And while we're on the subject of near-death experiences, I am scared to death of the kind of food we will have to eat. Nothing will be professionally cooked by health-inspected food preparers. We probably won't even pack hair nets for the food detail. Stuff cooked over an open fire or a camper stove is heavy on smoke, but light on fire. It's rare-meat city, Lord, salmonella waiting to happen.

"So I guess I just ask you one last time, Lord. Is there *any* way I can get out of this vacation without hurting my kids and my best friends? Please deliver the answer to me in the next twelve hours, so I can rest peacefully tonight.

"Amen.

"P.S. This pastor is wonderful, Lord. You brought a great guy to our flock."

I figured praising the pastor was worth a few extra points on God's great scale of "Should I answer this 'Yes' or 'No'?"

The prayer made me feel so much better. Being a man of faith, I just knew that God was going to deliver me from my hour of trial. After all, isn't this what a man of faith looks like in the nineties? We fully trust God to take care of everything we want. He is the God of convenience. He makes a career of bailing us out.

Sunday afternoon was dedicated to the task of packing. Both Tom and Edmund had gone out of their way to emphasize that we couldn't bring a lot of stuff. *Just pack the essentials* was the motto. "Think of it as a plane flight," Edmund stressed. "Limit yourself and all your kids to two carry-on items. Don't pack a lot of useless stuff you'll never need."

This advice was wise, but only up to a point. Consider Edmund's next comment: "By the way, there's no way to predict what kind of weather we'll have, so be prepared for everything from scorching sun to freezing rain."

I reduced all of Edmund's counsel to one sentence: *Pack everything you own into a backpack.* We certainly didn't want to look like a bunch of tourists with lots of luggage.

"All right, everybody!" I announced to my kids after lunch. "It's time to pack. Dig through the very depths of your bedroom closet and locate your suitcase. There will be lots of people on this trip, but very little room for luggage. So pack all the clothes you need to take in your suitcase. Then, pack your Game Boy, Walkman, and eight thousand cassettes in your backpack. Those are the only two articles Edmund will let us bring. You're all on your own."

This was a classic case of misplaced trust that would later explain why Bo wore the same T-shirt all week, and why Ben's socks got more pungent each day.

True to my self-sacrificial core, the key issue for me was what I was going to pack for myself:

—a Los Angeles Dodger cap in Dodger blue.

—a Los Angeles Dodger cap in tan with "L A" embroidered in Dodger blue.

—a Dallas Cowboy sweatshirt in navy blue.

—a Dallas Cowboy T-shirt in gray.

—a pair of Philadelphia Phillies sweatpants in red.

—a pair of gray Dodger sweatpants cut off.

—Cowboy Boxer shorts.

—Dodger briefs.

—a pair of Boston Celtics swim trunks.

Only one essential was not officially endorsed by the NFL, NBA, or Major League Baseball, and that was jeans. I threw a couple of pairs in my suitcase anyway.

After I finished packing for myself, I gingerly carried my suitcase out to the preassigned position on the front porch. It was heartwarming to see the five small, brown semi-Samsonite suitcases lined up all in a row. I had no idea what was inside of them, but the optimist in me imagined piles of spanking white underwear nestled between carefully folded shirts and pants.

The pessimist in me kept trying to tell me that every item in each suitcase was wadded into a wrinkled ball.

The plan was for the Grahams to drive their Winnebago. Edmund had rented a minivan to pull his tent trailer with, instead of his Lexus. However, Edmund is so hopelessly in love with his car, he couldn't part with it, so he allowed me to drive it as the third vehicle, instead of my Honda.

Six suitcases ready for action, I collapsed into my imitation-leather, Naugahyde recliner with the two bun indentions that beckoned me. No sooner had I picked up the remote and backed into the first recline position than the phone rang.

"Dad, it's for you," called Betsy.

"Yeah, right," I mocked, since it's never for me.

"It's Edmund, Dad!" she insisted.

"Well, what do you know?" It always amazes me that through the miraculous grace of God and the technology of AT&T, a phone call can still get through for me when I live with four teenagers.

"Hello, fellow camper, it's Edmund!" His voice boomed over the phone with the volume of a rescue squad siren.

"Edmund, you're coming through loud and clear, buddy," I said.

"We're about twelve hours from blastoff, so I just wanted to touch base with my fellow astronauts."

"Everything is A-OK here, partner," I replied mildly.

"Are you all packed?" he asked, suddenly turning serious.

"Yup, we're all packed!"

"Two suitcases per passenger?"

"Each of us has one suitcase and a backpack."

"So you'll all be ready to go tomorrow morning at 8:00 sharp?"

"That sounds great," I replied. "Hey, I should check everyone's packing list one last time. I'll see you tomorrow, okay?"

"Roger, my friend." He paused, apparently to look at his watch and do the math. "I'll see you in exactly eleven hours and forty-one minutes."

I didn't sleep much that night. Thanks to Edmund's astronaut motif, I had the weirdest dream that we were all in the Winnebago, we had run out of Tang, and Edmund kept screaming to passers-by on the highway, "Houston, we have a problem!"

✦

The first day of summer vacation is that glorious day when people can *sleep in.*

So what must my neighbors have thought when two large vehicles pulled up my street at precisely 8 a.m. and let loose with two air horns? Tom and Edmund saw that we were already waiting by the front door, yet they felt compelled to announce their arrival loud enough for our friends in Rio de Janeiro.

"Good morning, Butterworths!" Tom leaned out the window of his Winnebago, waving like an engineer in an old steam locomotive. Edmund was right behind him in his rented van, a tent trailer connected by steel and wires that looked to me like a camper's umbilical cord. Jenny was right behind Edmund driving in the newly washed Lexus.

Edmund tooted his horn one last time, causing our neighbors directly across the street to yell out an open upstairs window, "Keep it down out there! We're trying to sleep in!" Ducking as if he expected to be pelted with rotten tomatoes, Edmund slunk out of his van and tiptoed to our front porch.

"You guys are all ready to go. That's great!" Edmund's love affair with punctuality was far from secret. People always got along better with him if they showed up on time. As he popped the trunk of the Lexus, I took a good look at his vacation attire. CPA-casual, I concluded. Blue, button-down, short-sleeved collared shirt and khaki shorts. His old pair of sandals, once tan, were now

26

a well-worn brown highlighted by brand new sweat socks in gleaming, blinding white.

He had that look that no middle-aged man wanted to go for…Edmund looked like his father.

I remember how I wanted to hide when my Dad got out of the car to refill the gas tank after a few hours on the road toward our vacation destination. I'd pray and pray that we were far enough from home that no one would possibly recognize us.

By this time Tom had climbed down from the Winnebago to help us pack our stuff in the car. He came over just in time. We had already filled the trunk of the Lexus to overflowing and we still had three more bags to put in. "Here, let me give you guys a hand!" Tom offered kindly, as he began taking everything *out* of the trunk so that he could repack it properly.

"Why don't you guys say hello to the ladies over in the motor home and I'll be through here in a minute." This was clearly a signal from Tom that he didn't need the kind of help we could provide. I didn't feel too bad; after all, it wasn't my car. *Edmund's the one who should feel foolish, not being able to load his own trunk!* I sighed in relief, silently thanking God that Edmund was coming along. Ineptitude loves company.

Edmund and I go way back. Sometimes he has kept me from looking bad. And when he couldn't look worse than I did, he's helped me out of a lot of jams.

During the winter of 1988-89, we had more snow in Pine Woods than since I had moved in. Edmund drove his car up my driveway (he had a Mercedes back then, before he traded it in for the Lexus) and, of course, it was complete with snow chains. "Put your chains on, buddy, and I will follow you to work!" he offered. "That way I'll be certain you arrive all right. I'd hate to think of you stranded on the side of the road!"

Edmund's thoughts were touching indeed. Yet I knew they weren't completely selfless. After all, if I were stuck on the side of the road somewhere, the first person I'd call would be Edmund, so I guess he figured he'd rather help me now than have to bundle up and dig me out later.

I laid the chains out behind the tires, then backed over them. I bravely tried to hook the chains around the big, black, rubber doughnuts, but they just wouldn't link. But there was another issue here…I hadn't put snow chains on my car in fifteen years. There wasn't much about it that I could remember, other than it was a difficult job even when I was a lot younger.

Edmund kindly asked, "Could you use a little help, buddy?"

He squatted down in that cold, snowy driveway and proceeded to take over the impossible task of linking up those tire chains. At first he had gloves on, but they were too bulky and were soon shed. Before long Edmund's hands were bleeding from the attempts to hook those uncooperative links.

That was the day I learned how deep our friendship was.

That was also the day I learned the importance of buying tire chains that are the right size.

❖

I quickly eased over to the side door of Tom's monster Winnebago. True to his word, it was filled with females.

"Well, hi, Butterworths!" Meg Graham gushed. A beautiful lady, the kind that looked like she just stepped out of a catalog for Nordstrom's, Meg sparkled in her pink sleeveless blouse. Her hair was cut short and was as blonde as mine, with no hint of any gray or dark roots. She turned her head toward the back of the Winnebago, calling, "Girls, look who's here!"

Edmund's wife, Jenny, and their two daughters, Charlotte and Patti, came out from the back of the tin box on wheels. "Good morning, everyone," Jenny called. Probably ten years younger than Meg, Jenny had long brown hair and the whitest teeth I had ever seen on someone who wasn't posing for a toothpaste ad. She smiled at my kids, "Betsy, BJ, Brandon, Ben, Bo, you remember Charlotte and Patti, right?"

I watched as my kids smiled politely at Edmund's girls. My kids are older than Edmund's. Charlotte is ten and Patti is eight. As my kids looked on politely at his girls, I tried to read their minds:

—Betsy, my only daughter, winced inwardly. *Here we go, a week of for-free baby-sitting these two little girls while everyone else has fun!*
—BJ smiled and thought, *Hey, that Patti is cute…I wish she was ten years older!*
—Brandon, his father's son, smiled and thought, *Is that a box of Tastykakes right behind Charlotte on the counter by the microwave?*
—Ben smiled and thought, *Oh great! A week with two geeky girls! I hope no one expects me to spend any time with them!*
—Bo smiled, but being ten years old, he thought, *I gotta remember to hate girls, but I really think they're both total babes. So I guess I'll play it cool, and give them both a shot at the Bo-Man!*

Patti was clutching a Barbie doll tightly against her bright, multicolored top with matching multicolored shorts. "Anyone want to play Barbie with us?" she asked.

"Let's save that for another time," Jenny interrupted, sensing how unlikely it would be for four boys and a nineteen-year-old girl to turn somersaults over the invitation to play dolls.

"How about this game?" Meg interjected. As she spoke, she uncovered an old thirteen-inch television set, complete with all the attachments for video games.

"ALL RIGHT!" the kids sang in unison. Before we could say any more they were establishing the ground rules: who would play in what order, what games they would play in what order, how many levels a person could play before having to turn the controls over to another person.

"We're all ready!" Tom announced from the side door of the Winnebago. "So who wants to ride in here?"

"I DO!" all the kids screamed.

"Well, okay, that's fine," he stammered. Tom hadn't felt so popular since he retired from baseball.

"Can I still drive the Winnebagel?" Edmund asked like an eager schoolboy.

"Do you really think you can handle it?" Tom started to perspire underneath his PING visor.

"Yes, sir." Edmund answered.

"Okay, you can drive it for the first hour of our trip, then we'll stop in order to assess the situation."

"Tom and I will drive in the van pulling the tent trailer," Meg concluded, firmly clutching her husband's massive right hand. That hand had thrown out many players when Tom was a Dodger. I didn't even want to consider what that hand could do to Edmund if he were to somehow screw up while driving Tom's expensive tin box.

"I'll drive the Lexus," I said, stating the obvious.

"By yourself?" Meg asked. Her big blue eyes got all sad and droopy. She made riding alone sound like a fifty-year stint in a maximum security prison.

"Nonsense," Jenny interjected. "I'll drive with Bill, if that's okay with you, Edmund."

"Sure, no problem," Edmund sang. "I've got plenty of company with Charlotte, Patti, Betsy, BJ, Brandon, Ben, and Bo!"

"I've got something I want to talk to you about, anyway," added Jenny.

I didn't like the sound of this, and my stomach instantly tightened into all the knots in the Boy Scout handbook.

CHAPTER THREE

We lined up our vehicles in order of size, a convoy version of the Three Bears. Edmund led the caravan in Papa Bear Rig with a half dozen bicycles bungee-corded to the back and a stack of folding chairs bungeed to the roof.

What did we do before the advent of the bungee cord? Is there an inventor somewhere, some man named Boris Bungee or woman named Beatrice Bungee, to whom we should pay homage for solving the age-old dilemma of how to hold things together?

Without bungee cords the gate on my fence wouldn't close, the lid to the steamer trunk that sits in my garage wouldn't shut, and I couldn't hang up socks to dry in my shower.

I settled into the luxurious leather upholstery in the Holmeses' black ES 300. The climate control was set to seventy-two degrees, the CD player was singing a James Taylor compact disc out of its eight speakers. I set the cruise control for a law-abiding fifty-five miles per hour. Driving was so effortless in this dream machine, I would have dozed off had it not been for Jenny.

"So how are all the kids doing?"

"Fine."

"How's Betsy doing?"

"Fine."

"I know you're real proud of her."

"Real proud," I repeated.

"So it's you and the four boys for another year."

"I guess so."

There was a pause, longer than usual, and I suspected trouble. I was correct.

"Bill, forgive me if this is out of line, but you need a *woman* in that house."

"Tell me about it," I lamented.

"How long have you been single again?"

I had to think for a moment. I'd done a pretty good job of blocking out the darkest day of my life—when my wife left me. "Let's see," I finally said, "It's been almost four years."

"It's time," Jenny pronounced, as if she were Dr. Jenny, Noted Psychotherapist and Relationship Guru with books, tapes, videos, and her own infomercial.

Another long pause convinced me that I was getting closer and closer to a highway I had driven before...*Blind Date Boulevard.*

"I know someone who would be perfect for you."

"Ahh, Jenny, I don't know... ."

"Wait, Bill, let me finish," she pushed. "She's a few years younger than you."

"That's good."

"She has a wonderful personality," she continued.

Of course, "She has a wonderful personality" is where it always starts, I noted with a trace of sarcasm.

"She's a deeply committed Christian."

"Well, actually that *is* very important to me."

"She holds down a good job."

"Ahh, perhaps I could marry into wealth," I teased.

It appeared that Jenny was finished with her description of this person. But I had more questions still left unanswered.

"Sooo, what does she look like?" I finally asked the question men aren't supposed to care about, but do.

Jenny's countenance lit up like a Roman candle. "Oh, so we are *interested,* are we?"

"I don't know."

"Oh yes you do know, or you wouldn't have asked what she looked like." Jenny tossed back her long brown hair and stared ahead in a look of confident victory. After leaving me in suspense for another three or four miles, she answered my question. "Well there are some pretty significant people who think she is extremely attractive."

"What people?" I asked.

"The judges of the Miss Orange County Contest."

"What?"

"That's right. She was chosen Miss Orange County several years ago."

"How long ago is *several* years ago?" I asked, swallowing hard.

"Don't push it, Bill," Jenny scolded. "Remember I said she was younger than you."

"Oh. Right. I forgot."

"Did you know that Michelle Pfeiffer is a former Miss Orange County?"

"No, I didn't."

"Well, she is," Jenny was gloating by now. "I'll just let you think about that for a moment."

I was imagining Michelle Pfeiffer with just a few more years on her, serving God, making a good living, and being single and available to a jolly soul like me. I liked the picture.

"What's her name?" I asked.

"Jessica."

"That's pretty. What's her last name?"

"I'm glad you like her first name," Jenny said hesitantly.

"What did you say her last name was?" I repeated the question.

After a long breath Jenny responded. "Her name is Jessica Quaggenblocker."

"*Quaggenblocker?* What kind of last name is Quaggenblocker?"

Wanting nothing to get in the way of her matchmaking, Jenny quickly countered, "Think of it this way, Bill. She's got to be dying to change her last name!"

"That's a good point," I mused. "But I'm not sure I'd measure up to the expectations of a former Miss Orange County."

"Nonsense," Jenny countered. "You're a wonderful man."

"Right," I scoffed. "You have to say that because you're my best friend's wife!"

"That's not true," she scolded. "You have many marvelous traits. You're a terrific father, a great speech teacher, you genuinely care about other people, you really love the Lord, and you're a great listener—a far too rare thing in a man! Oh, and I almost forgot, you're a great friend. What would Edmund do without you?"

"Add that I would make the ideal Cub Scout," I mocked, red-faced with embarrassment.

"So, are you interested?"

"Even if I was, Jenny, I've got five kids to take care of. What woman in her right mind would be interested in a guy with five children?"

"Jessica Quaggenblocker would!"

"How can you be so sure?" I asked.

"Because I've already asked her," Jenny blurted out.

"*You did?*" I screamed, nearly swerving off the road. As Jenny and I climbed back off the front dash, I noted that these brakes were much quicker than my Honda's.

Jenny, nonplussed, rubbed her forehead and continued. "Yes, I did ask her," she said. "As a matter of fact, she's *very* interested in meeting you."

"Well, maybe *someday* we can set up something," I said.

"Guess where she lives now?" Jenny kept prodding.

"I have no idea. Casablanca?"

"Don't be silly, Bill. She lives in San Luis Obispo."

"How nice," I stated matter-of-factly.

"You know that's only ten miles from where we're going to be camping," Jenny said, her brown eyes widening in expectation of my response.

"How convenient," I muttered.

"I'll bet while we're camping, Meg and I could watch your kids so you could slip away in order to spend a little time with Jessica." Jenny made it sound like a heart-pounding romance.

"You've got this all figured out, don't you?"

"Well, Meg and I did put our heads together a little bit," she cooed.

"I really do appreciate how you are looking out for me." I gently patted her hand.

"So you'll go out with her?"

I felt extremely awkward, so I decided to answer her the way I answer 85 percent of the questions my kids ask me.

"We'll see, Jenny. We'll see."

❈

Edmund allowed Tom to pass him and lead the way off the exit on Interstate 5 just below Stockton. We found an Exxon service station and proceeded to pull in, Papa, Mama, and Baby Bear, into the side area of the station.

"Dad, this Winnebagel is the coolest thing in the world!" Bo shouted excitedly from the window on the right side. "Can we get one, Dad?"

"Sure. Right after I buy that small Greek island I've been in the market for," I answered.

"It really is something, buddy!" Edmund agreed as he emerged from Tom's new toy. "You'll have to give it a spin sometime!"

"What about now?" came a voice from behind me. Tom had just finished inspecting the motor home from top to bottom, front to back.

"Oh, I didn't mean right now!" Edmund protested.

"I think now is the perfect time for Bill to take the wheel," Tom answered emphatically. "He can drive the middle leg and then I'll drive the last leg into Happy Clam State Park."

"Gee, guys, I don't know…" Now it was *my* turn to protest. I had never even considered that they would want *me* to drive this two-story colonial on wheels.

"There's nothing to it," Tom said comfortingly as he put his arm around my shoulder and walked me away from the others. When we were a safe distance from other ears, he confessed his fears in shocking transparency.

"Bill, I'm gonna shoot straight with you. Edmund is a world-class guy, no doubt about it. But behind the wheel of my motor home…frankly, he frightens me."

"I see," was about all I could squeak out.

"So I *need* you to drive—do you understand?"

"I guess I do."

"I need you to do this for the safety of my Winnebago. I'm really counting on you, brother. Will you do it, man?"

I felt like Vince Lombardi was preparing to send me in as linebacker on a third and inches. Could I even think about telling him that I'd rather not play?

I squared my shoulders. "I'll do it, Tom," I answered.

"Great!" Tom patted me on the back and led me to the motor home for some last-minute instructions.

"Yikes, this thing is big!" I commented as I got closer and closer to my destiny. I had trouble maneuvering my Honda. How was I gonna steer this aircraft carrier?

"There's one main thing you've got to remember," Tom began. "When you make a left-hand turn, your back end is going to swing out about an extra three feet."

As he said that, I envisioned walking down the street and turning left while my rear end inflated an extra three feet in circumference.

"Stay with me, brother!" Tom exhorted. "Let me go over it one more time. When you turn left, the back end of the motor home will swing out three feet beyond the front. It's what we call the *swing radius*."

Moments later, with seven kids seated behind me, oblivious to a man about to have a seizure, I turned the key, gave it a little gas, let it return to idle, and put it into gear.

Since I was now Papa Bear, I had to lead the way. I chose to exit out the rear of the service station so I wouldn't have to put the motor home in reverse. The first exercise would test my resolve. I had to turn left in order to exit the Exxon.

I checked my mirrors and all appeared clear. There was a parked car on my right, but it wasn't close enough to affect my turn. I proceeded carefully, methodically.

1. I pulled forward another six feet.
2. I put on my left turn signal.

3. I checked both mirrors—all was clear.

4. I turned left to exit the service station.

5. The back end of the Winnebago took off a very large piece of the car that was parked far away enough not to affect my turn.

The good news was that it was an old car. The bad news was that I took most of it with me out the exit.

When I slammed on my brakes, I could hear Edmund and then Tom do the same.

Everyone stepped from his or her respective vehicle and we met in unison in the middle of the parking lot. Each person seemed to have his or her own agenda.

Tom was first to speak: "Bill, are you all right?"

Followed by Jenny: "Charlotte, Patti, are you two okay?"

Meg: "Bill, are your kids all safe?"

Then my best friend, Edmund: "You forgot about the swing radius, you ding-dong!"

Finally, a man with eyes bugged out and a key to the men's room in his hand said: "What has happened to my car? This is a classic! I'm not sure it can be replaced!"

I swallowed hard. *Just my luck, I hit a clunker and the owner is going to say it was a priceless classic.*

Tom kept reassuring me that everything was going to be all right. As long as no one was hurt, he kept telling me, it was no big deal. I really wanted to believe him, but I had my doubts.

The California Highway Patrol was summoned, accident reports filed, and witness accounts heard. I silently asked God to remove me from this scene if it were at all possible. Worse than Edmund's constant digs about how stupid I was to crash into a parked car was the look in Tom's eyes that said, *I thought Edmund was the stupid one!*

Granted, the Winnebago suffered little damage. But I had let Tom down. He called everyone together one last time as we regrouped for the remainder of the trip. Edmund was assigned to drive the van, taking along with him BJ, Brandon, Ben, and Bo for guy-talk. Jenny was told to drive the Lexus with Betsy for company. Tom said he and Meg would lead the way in the motor home.

After all the assignments were made, Tom motioned me to my new position for the rest of the trip.

I rode in the back of the Winnebago with Charlotte and Patti.

❖

By the time we arrived on the central California coast, I was relieved to be playing Barbie with Charlotte and Patti. It was fitting that I was reduced to easier life decisions: should Barbie wear her hair in one ponytail or two?

About ten miles past San Luis Obispo, we exited off of Highway 101 at a sign that said, *Exit for Happy Clam Beach, Arroyo Grande, Shell Beach, Oceano and Grover City.* We turned right and drove down a stretch of winding road.

"There's a sign!" Meg suddenly sang out to Tom as she pointed to her right. It was her job as navigator to alert Tom of approaching landmarks, signposts, and historical points of interest. The sign to which she referred simply read *The Happy Clam State Park* with an arrow pointing to the right.

"I see it!" Tom sounded as if he were a Pilgrim on the *Mayflower* who just discovered a roasted turkey dinner on top of Plymouth Rock. "We're almost there, kids!"

Charlotte and Patti started whooping and hollering and jumping up and down. Normally, I would tolerate such behavior, but in their childlike recklessness, they completely ruined the darling

41

living area I had set up for my Barbie and Ken. I tried to hold back my scowl.

⬧

We left the Lexus out by the road so we wouldn't be charged for the extra vehicle. We pulled the other two vehicles into Row L where two spaces awaited our entry. I watched with envy as Tom backed the Winnebago into a spot that I couldn't have negotiated with a moped. Edmund was doing the same thing with the tent trailer. I stood with the women, children, and Barbies—my newly discovered peer group.

"Can I get my luggage?" I asked, not wanting to be a part of any of the backbreaking set-up work that I assumed was coming up. Plus my stomach was churning down Acid Avenue.

"You sure can," Tom answered. He paused and started shaking his head. "Actually we should have brought it with us, but we left it all out in the Lexus. Tell you what, buddy," Tom continued. "I'll get the bikes down off the motor home and you and your kids can ride out to get your stuff. How does that sound?"

"Great!" my kids answered on my behalf, although not necessarily the way I would have.

The bikes unbungeed, Tom suggested that three of us ride on the seats, while the other three rode on our handlebars. "That way, you'll have three people to carry luggage while the other three pedal back on their bikes!"

Brandon, BJ, and I mounted the bikes provided for us. Bo hopped on Brandon's handlebars, Betsy jumped on BJ's.

"Do I have to ride with Dad?" Ben asked.

"Looks like it," Betsy answered, a note of pity in her voice.

"Have you ridden a bike lately?" BJ asked, becoming aware of the concern among his siblings.

"Of course!" I answered confidently, trying to remember.

"You sure, Dad?" Ben asked, knowing it was his carcass on the line, or on the handlebars, as it were.

"You're safe with me, Ben," I assured.

"That's what he said to me right before he knocked me out of the golf cart on the fourteenth hole at Pine Woods Country Club," BJ said with a laugh as he drove off with Betsy on his handlebars.

"Come on, Ben, we'll show 'em." I gritted my teeth and started down the path.

"Should I get on first, Dad?" Ben asked innocently, watching me pass him.

"Whoops!" I cried, "almost forgot my cargo." I stopped, allowed his long, lanky, fourteen-year-old body to drape itself all over the bicycle, and pushed hard on the pedals.

I couldn't get that bike to budge.

"Ready, Dad?" Ben inquired.

"I...can't...seem...to...get...the...bike...moving," I huffed and puffed through vain efforts to produce motion from the pedals.

"Let me try to ride you," Ben said, adding insult to injury.

"Oh, Benjamin, get real. If I can't move us, surely you can't move us."

"Well, we're going nowhere like this, so let me try. It can't hurt anything, can it?"

I shrugged my shoulders, dismounted, and watched him get in position.

"Okay, Dad, hop on." I awkwardly attempted to get my overweight body on the handlebars. After two attempts, I scaled the mountain.

"Here we go, Dad!" Ben said with true joy. With a mixture of fright, shock, and exhilaration, I witnessed the unthinkable. Ben was riding me on his handlebars! We were moving! We were even going in the right direction!

"I can't believe you can do this, Benjamin!" I exclaimed, feeling relieved for the first time since we'd left that morning. "This is gonna be a great vacation," I said in a choked whisper.

"That's the attitude, Dad," Ben quipped happily from his seat of power.

It was just what I needed to snap me out of my anticamping funk. We reached the Lexus a few minutes later. I was spending quality time with my kids. At this particular juncture, quality time took some rather unusual forms:

—Waiting by the Lexus an extra half hour, since none of us remembered to bring the car keys. Brandon graciously volunteered to go back for them, leaving me with the other four on this desolate stretch of road.

—Walking back to the motor home with my arms full of suitcases, BJ and Ben following me, as Betsy, Brandon, and Bo pedaled slowly alongside, offering moral support.

For a few hours, I was a fun father. We may have looked like a ragged band of vagabonds in search of food and shelter, but we joked and laughed as if we were rich. The suitcases didn't feel heavy, and we barely noticed the sticky heat.

Not only did we have fun on our journey through the Land of Luggage, but upon our return we discovered that the Winnebago and tent trailer were all set up. Awnings, folding chairs, barbecue pits, bicycles, and sunscreens—I kept looking for the portable hot tub.

Everyone was working hard at relaxing.

Unfortunately, in my bliss, I had overlooked one glaring fact. I still had to pitch the tent our family was staying in.

Chapter Four

The Grahams were settled in at 90210 Heights, the Holmes were settled in at Bungalow Drive. It was time for the Butterworths to settle in on the western outskirts of Tent City, also known as Bug Flats.

"You'll do well, I know you will!" Tom said in his manly voice as he handed me the tent gear.

"He doesn't have a clue what he's doing," Edmund clucked his tongue and smirked.

I glared at Edmund, secretly wishing my stares were burning laser beams. "We'll be just fine," I said.

I wanted to believe Tom, but I had this scary feeling that Edmund was prophetic.

Just the same, Edmund's comments stung. This was the guy who came to my rescue the summer afternoon I wrapped an entire spool of plastic twine from my weed-whacker around my body. I thought the thing was unplugged. I looked inside to see how it worked, and next thing I knew I was face down in my backyard, whimpering like a baby. Edmund heard my moans, hopped the fence, and within minutes had me untied, thanks to his Swiss army knife that all bean counters conceal in their perma-press gabardine pockets.

So why was this guy so snide with me now? *Maybe I should confront him like it says in Matthew,* I thought. Then another voice said, *Don't make a mountain out of a molehill,* a catchy passage I think I might've read in the Bible somewhere. What right had I to ask Edmund about his rudeness? I would suffer it nobly, as right-eous persecution. I would not notice the speck in my brother's eye—plus, it would be easier.

Tom and Edmund handed me a duffel bag that contained all the gear necessary to pitch the tent our family would be using. So with the kids behind me, I took off for a little walk through the campgrounds on my way to our tent-pitching location on the beach.

As I shuffled through the facility, my five camping disciples behind me, I couldn't help but notice the "stalls" (I hate that word). Parked in them were every imaginable contraption, all grouped under the general heading "campers." Some motor homes looked typical, only a few years old, clean, orderly, and rep-resenting the middle of the line in these sorts of vehicles.

But others made even the Grahams' Winnebago look like an old, beat-up refrigerator box on four used bicycle tires. These mansions on wheels were long, sleek, and shiny. They had all the latest bells and whistles and must have cost as much as a house in Indiana. Their tanned owners sat outside their castles on brand-new chaise lounges thickly padded with red-and-white-striped cushions. They sipped iced tea from frosted tumblers while read-ing a *New York Times* best-seller through three-hundred-dollar Italian sunglasses. Some further flaunted their wealth by parking their brand new Mercedes right next to the motor home as opposed to outside the campgrounds.

"This must be how Bill Gates, Steven Spielberg, and Michael Jackson camp out!" I mumbled to myself. "I wonder if these folks travel with butlers and maids?"

But even more shocking were the motor homes that looked like they'd come for an Ugliest Motor Home Contest. To say these campers were run down is like calling a teenager's bedroom slightly disheveled. Besides dents, rust, peeling paint, life-choking exhaust problems, oil burning, and fender hanging, there were several motor homes that weren't pretty at all. Their owners wore smelly, ripped-up, sleeveless T-shirts that were too small for them, and their guts protruded six or seven inches past their cut-off shorts. The only way to rid them of their beer cans would be through surgery.

Of course, there were also tent trailers of every imaginable description. I thought of Edmund whenever I came to a shining silver trailer. I wondered why he hadn't gotten one of these shocking space-like campers to complete his astronaut dream? The answer came to me in one word...Jenny.

As the kids and I walked along the road, the heat soaked my shirt and sweat poured out from under my hat, creating a neat and even waterfall-type effect on my forehead. My punishment for all the sins I had ever committed was all wadded up in a blue duffel bag that I carried toward the beach. My mind raced with unanswered questions. *How could such a tiny bag hold a tent big enough for six of us to sleep in? Did Miss Quaggenblocker like Tastykakes? Did tents come with directions? Could earwigs survive beach conditions?*

Driving all these questions was the biggest one: *How could I come off as a macho-male, together kind of guy, camper extraordinaire, when I barely knew how to work a weed-whacker?*

And what about this blind-date thing? Did I really want to go through the emotional roller coaster of meeting a total stranger?

What if she liked me, but I didn't like her? Or worse, what if I liked her, but she didn't like me? What if I fell head over heels in love with this woman, only to find out she's already engaged to a dashingly handsome former pro wrestler who is now a millionaire in the computer industry?

Continuing west, we left the confines of the campground, walked up a small hill, and discovered the sand dunes on the other side. A long stretch of the dunes was covered in a quilt of ice plant, a strange green growth that is crunchy to walk on. The boys quickly discovered how to crush the plants with their feet to make a sound similar to bodily emissions.

"I feel like I am inside a giant burp," Betsy complained to me as the boys ran ahead in their quest for the perfect-sounding ice plant.

"Any suggestions?" I asked weakly.

"Yeah, how about four sisters instead of four brothers?" she replied.

"Do you know anything about how to set up a tent?" I quizzed. "Perhaps this is something you learned down at college in Los Angeles?"

"Not really," she answered. "I wouldn't call L.A. the rugged camper capitol of the world. Although I do know that it's called 'pitching' a tent, Dad, not 'setting it up.'"

"Oh yeah. I knew that," I lied.

"Why didn't Tom or Edmund offer to come out and help us?" Betsy asked inquisitively.

"That's a fair question," I replied. "They both said setting up this tent would be a good initiation into the world of camping."

"Pitching, Dad."

"Whatever." (I had to admit, whenever I heard the word "pitching," my mind went to Todd Worrell, ace Dodger reliever.)

Betsy proceeded cautiously. "Dad, were they sorta laughing when they said all this to you?"

"Yeah, kinda," I recalled reluctantly.

"Have you *ever* pitched a tent before, Dad?" Betsy asked.

"No, I can't say that I have," I admitted dejectedly. Seeing how this depressed her, I quickly added, "But I think I saw a special on it once during a PBS marathon."

"Weren't you in the Boy Scouts when you were a kid?" she asked, hopefully.

"Yes, I was."

"Didn't you learn how to pitch a tent back then?"

"Well, no, actually I never learned."

"Why not?"

"Don't you remember?" I responded, becoming increasingly irritated. "I've told you before. I never went on their camping trips because I had that little problem."

"Oh, that's right," she said, the light going on in her head. "Except for sleeping in your bedroom, you were afraid of the dark when you were a little kid."

"Sort of," was all I could say.

I could see her mind recalling a scene I had recounted to her. I was staying over at a friend's house and we had decided to sleep out in his backyard. Midway through the night, I awoke to the unfamiliar setting and proceeded to snap. The fear of the dark, coupled with the reality of being outside in my Roy Rogers footie pajamas, was too much for this little boy to handle. I began screaming like I was the latest victim of the Boston Strangler. I remember the neighbors said they never heard a voice so loud. I also remember I was never invited over there again.

"I'm sorry, Daddy," Betsy apologized compassionately. "I didn't mean to bring up anything embarrassing." She leaned over, kissed me on the forehead, and hugged me tightly.

"That's okay," I hugged her back. "It's no big deal. Anyway, it's not a problem anymore."

I hoped.

◼

The Pacific Ocean roared its greeting to us as we dropped the duffel bag next to the chosen spot for our tent. We found a space relatively clear of ice plants, despite the complaints of the boys, who apparently wanted to play "Burp Impersonation" the entire night. The ground was sandy but appeared firm enough to hold our tent stakes.

By now the four boys and Betsy had all gathered around me to observe the ceremonial Dumping of the Duffel. Unzipping the blue bag, I turned it upside down, spilling its contents all over the ground. It was uncanny to me that our home away from home was entirely contained in the pile of canvas, ropes, and plastic that littered the beach.

The foolish man builds his house upon the sand kept running through my mind. "My life verse!" I muttered.

"What's that, Pops?" BJ asked.

"Nothing, BJ, just mumbling to myself."

"Where did we get this tent, Dad?" Brandon inquired, as he kicked around the contents on the ground with his hundred-dollar, rubber-cushioned, Air Jordan Nikes.

"It's Tom's. I don't know where he got it."

"I do," he laughed, as he continued to poke around in the soon-to-be-tent. "Look at this!"

He turned over the largest piece of canvas, which I took to be the tent itself. It was blue, matching the duffel bag. Brandon had discovered a marking on the side of the canvas.

"It's the Dodgers logo!" Bo shouted as the kids all cheered in unison.

"Not only did Tom used to play for the Dodgers," I added with pride, "but he used to camp with them!"

"Maybe Todd Worrell has slept in this very tent!" Bo exclaimed.

"Maybe he did!" I liked the idea as much as Bo. "But what's really helpful," I added, "is that this logo probably goes on the outside of the tent, so now we have a clue as to the positioning of the canvas."

The kids just smiled and nodded. They had no idea what I was talking about.

"Where do we begin, Dad?" Ben asked.

"Let's make sure we have everything," I suggested, not really knowing where to begin myself. "See these little yellow plastic thingamajigs?" I asked, pointing to the six-inch-long rods while demonstrating an extraordinary grasp of camping lingo.

"The stakes?" BJ clarified.

"Right, the stakes," I said, logging a new word into my vocabulary. (Although I must admit, when he said "stakes," I immediately thought of *steaks*.)

"What about them?" BJ asked.

"Let's put them all into one big pile, so we're sure we have enough of them."

"Okay, Dad. Whatever you say." The kids were silently looking at one another with pained expressions.

Brandon had already begun putting small pieces of pole together into one tall pole. "This will be in the center of the tent, Dad," he said with authority.

"Have you done this before?" I asked excitedly.

"No," he responded matter-of-factly, "but it just takes common sense to come up with that little discovery."

Ah yes, common sense! *I must have left that at home also.*

"I'll start hammering in the tent pegs, if someone will hand me the hammer," BJ volunteered, sensing it was time for the kids to take charge while Dad wandered in the wilderness of ignorance.

"Dad? The hammer? Do you have the hammer?" He waved his hands in front of my eyes trying furiously to get my attention back toward our dilemma.

"A hammer?" I asked perceptively.

"Yeah, you know, wooden handle, steel head, use it to pound things into other things," BJ sounded sarcastic, yet I was such a tool-dunce, I wondered if he wasn't trying to be helpful.

"I know what a hammer is, BJ," I said, "I just don't know where one is."

We all started combing through the contents of our campsite-in-a-sack. There were lots of fun things to kick around, but the fun stopped short of a hammer.

"We didn't bring a hammer?" Ben spoke in a tone of voice that sounded like we forgot food and water.

"I saw one in Tom's motor home," Bo remembered, trying to be helpful.

"Okay, I'll go back to get it," BJ volunteered.

"Thanks, son," I said politely. But inside, I felt abandoned. BJ occasionally looked like he knew what he was doing, whereas I never gave that impression.

"We can tie the cords to the pegs and the tent while we're waiting," Brandon suggested.

"That's a great idea, Brandon!"

We all felt the same way about Brandon taking some leadership. Like a family of beavers, we busily gathered around the twigs and sticks that would eventually become our dam. But there were too many beavers for any sort of effective work, and before too long, we were tripping over each other.

"I forgot to bring my pillow and sleeping bag over from the campgrounds," Bo mumbled innocently as we played with cords and stakes and canvas in a desperate attempt to give the impression that we knew what we were doing.

"None of us brought our stuff over yet, Bo," Betsy answered. "We've got to go back to get it once we pitch the tent."

"You know," I mused, "some of you could head on back to get that stuff now, if you want to. It appears we have more helpers than we need, especially since we're all waiting for the hammer, anyway."

"Okay," Betsy answered, taking the hint. "Bo, do you want to walk back to the campground with me and we'll get the blankets and pillows and sleeping bags?"

"Sure," he answered.

"Ben, do you want to go with us?" she asked.

"I don't know."

"I think you should." Betsy gave him that look that said, *Come with us and come with us now.*

"Okay, I'll go," he said.

Betsy turned my way and continued with the plan, "Do you think over the next fifteen minutes you and Brandon and BJ can put this tent together for us?"

"We'll certainly try our best," I answered, fully realizing what was going on here. Betsy, the always-perceptive one in our household, was doing her best to minimize my embarrassment. Granted, a child should see his father's humanity, but on the other hand, a father should be modest about his humanity. The less a kid sees his dad botch, the better off.

So, with Betsy, Ben, and Bo off to the campground, BJ not yet back with the hammer, it left Brandon and me alone, pondering the intimidating task before us.

"I really think we can do this, Dad," Brandon said in an unusual show of encouragement.

"I appreciate your attitude, buddy," I said with genuine sincerity. But the truth was, I was worried. I certainly didn't know what I was doing, and as positive as Brandon was, it was pretty clear to me that he didn't know either.

Once again I was left with no other recourse...I had to beseech the Lord.

"Dear God," I started praying in a silent panic, "we really need you here. You are the Wonderful Counselor. You are the Prince of Peace. You are the Everlasting Father. You are the Bread of Life. You are the Good Shepherd. You are the Great Physician. There are so many profound and wonderful titles for you. I was just wondering...since you used to live in the Tabernacle—do you still remember how to pitch a tent?

"If so, could you demonstrate right here on the beach, Lord? That's familiar turf for you, right? You helped out Moses in a big way when he was stuck on the beach by the Red Sea. You walked on water in Galilee. You caused the fishermen's nets to be filled on the sea. Could you just do one more seaside miracle? Could you help us pitch this tent? Please? Amen."

I stared at the potential tent, still collapsed on the ground, wondering if God would hear my prayer.

Maybe we're in the wrong hemisphere, I thought. *I guess you gotta be over in the Holy Land for beach-related miracles to occur.*

"Why are you staring at the tent and mumbling?" Brandon asked.

"Nothing," I answered.

"Well," he went on, "while you were off in La-La land, something very incredible has happened!" His confident smile assured me that he wasn't kidding.

"What are you talking about?"

Without a word, he turned to his left, pointing to a spot about a hundred feet down the beach. I followed his index finger to God's answer to my prayer. Another family was pitching a tent that appeared to be exactly like ours. And best of all, they were campers! They clearly knew what they were doing!

"It's a miracle!" I uttered, feeling like I should immediately fall prostrate on the sand.

"Easy, Dad," Brandon urged.

"No, you don't understand. It really is a miracle! I had just prayed to God to help us pitch the tent! Instead of raising it up by himself, he brought this other family onto the beach so we could watch them. We'll just do what they do, and we'll have the tent up in no time. This family is from heaven itself!"

"Actually, their car is right over there and the license plate says they're from Nebraska, but I know what you mean," Brandon teased. "Anyway, I think you're right. It is a miracle. Look more closely at that family. Not only do they know what they're doing, but they also have a teenage daughter who is *fine*. There is a God."

Brandon's relationship with the Lord was on a different plane than mine, but whether it was tent-pitching instructions or fine teenage girls, at that moment we both had to agree with the New Testament teaching that every good and perfect gift comes from above.

We watched in silent awe as they pitched their tent. I even found a pencil and an old Burger King napkin in order to scribble down some notes concerning the procedure. By the time BJ was back with the hammer, we knew what we were doing.

The three of us hammered tent-pegs, placed poles into the sleeves of canvas, tied knots, and before long, our tent was pitched.

It was an emotional moment for me. Seeing the white Dodger logo on the side of our blue canvas tent, now standing tall and secure, a lump formed in my throat and wetness filled my eyes. A son on either side of me, this was like some climactic movie scene when the mountain climbers stand shoulder to shoulder on the highest peak.

"We did it, boys, we did it," I barely choked out.

They smiled and put their arms over my shoulders. Actually, they had done it, while I proudly watched. Between God and my sons, I was really quite an impressive dad.

This slice of time would be important to remember when all heck would later break loose in the tent of miracles.

CHAPTER FIVE

The six of us marched back to Happy Clam Campgrounds with an air of dignity and panache. After all, we had pitched a tent—a feat never before attempted by a Butterworth. This is what family vacation memories are all about. It felt so good to have transformed a duffel bag full of puzzle pieces into a shelter for my family. I felt like the Great Protector, the Macho Male, the Davy Crockett of all frontiersmen.

"Well, look who's back!" Edmund announced to his family as he saw us approaching his tent trailer. "It took you guys longer than I thought it would," he continued.

"Longer?" I asked.

"Sure," he said, glancing down at his digital watch. "I thought you guys would be back here begging for help about forty-five minutes ago!"

"AH HA!" I screamed like Columbo solving the mystery. "You sent us off to the beach alone because you thought we couldn't pitch a tent without your help!" I glared at Edmund as he flashed what I took to be a wicked smile of tacit agreement.

"I must admit, I was having a little fun with you all," Edmund made it sound so innocent, putting on that expression that reminded me of a gassy baby.

The thought of Edmund purposely scheming up a plan to embarrass me in front of my children stuck in my mind like a piece of gristle lodged between two molars. This was the same guy who had prepared my tax statements for the last ten years. The first five years I was making so little money, he was such a caring friend, he did it for free!

"Well, I've got news for you, Mr. Smarty-pants!" I announced to my best friend.

"Oh yeah?" he barked back.

"For your information, we pitched the tent all by ourselves." I stopped speaking in order to allow the full force of that statement to hit Edmund. "Hear what I'm saying, old buddy? We didn't need your help in any way, shape, or form!"

Now it was my turn to smile the smile of the unrighteous.

Edmund turned to my kids in utter disbelief. "Is your dad trying to pull my leg? Did he really pitch the tent?"

"We pitched the tent, Uncle Edmund," Brandon responded in a tactically beautiful move to protect his father. Granted, I didn't do much more than watch as my boys pitched the tent, but this was no time to squabble over minor technicalities. Blood was thicker than tent pegs. It was time for family unity. Time for all the Butterworths to circle the wagons.

The Great Outdoors apparently pits family against family in a challenge for survival, so it was exhilarating to see my kids fearlessly take on Edmund like he was a bullying Goliath. Oh, how proud I was to feel Butterworth cholesterol coursing through my veins.

The loud voices that Edmund and I were using had attracted the attention of Jenny and the girls, as well as Tom and Meg. They all bounded out of their respective camping cocoons at the same time, clearly concerned about the ruckus.

"Edmund, what's going on here?" Jenny demanded in a voice clearly reserved for a wife dressing down her husband. Her stern stare could have stupored Superman.

"He's being a jerk, that's what's going on." Edmund moved a step closer, pointing his index finger at me, then poking my chest.

"Knock it off!" I yelled back, brushing his bony little finger away from me like you'd swat a fly. "Don't touch me like that again, either, or I may be forced to clean your clock!" I was so angry, I started saying words that had never found their way out of my mouth before. Suddenly I felt guilty about watching so many reruns of *The Rockford Files*. It was rubbing off. I was talking to my best friend like I lived in a trailer on Malibu Beach and drove a gold Pontiac Firebird.

"Hey, guys, relax!" Tom stepped between the two sides like he must have done a hundred times in his baseball career so the game could proceed. "There's no reason for either of you to be upset, so why don't we just cool off a little bit, okay?"

Meg was right behind him, nodding in nervous agreement. Jenny stood to the right of Edmund, her hands on her hips, tapping her toe in the dirt, not sure whose side to take. Charlotte and Patti glared at my kids, who, in true Christian charity, glared right back at them.

"We're gonna need some wood for the campfire tonight down on the beach." Tom continued to work at negotiating the peace process by tactfully changing the subject. "Bill, how about if you and your kids gather up some wood for our evening time together?"

It was the camper's equivalent to running laps after you messed around in Phys. Ed. class. "You guys go ahead and take ten laps around the track!"

"I wanna get some wood!" Patti whined from behind her father, formerly known as Edmund, but from now on our family will call him The Happy Clam Bully.

"Me, too," Charlotte complained, doing her best to support the Holmes version of family unity. Edmund's daughters were really starting to get on my nerves. I must admit I was still ticked at them for not sharing all their stuff when we were playing Barbies in the back of the motor home.

"One can never have too much firewood, can one?" Meg interjected.

Why weren't the women fighting? Isn't it usually the females who are given to this sort of bickering? Since when did men get so confrontational?

"Never too much firewood, that's right, Meg," Tom chuckled, picking up on the theme of peace at any price. "All of you can gather firewood together. It'll be a fun time of camaraderie."

"Can we split up?" Edmund asked, his tone reflecting his continued hostility.

"All right," Tom agreed.

"Fine," Edmund continued. "We'll go north of the campgrounds, and the Butterworths can go south. We'll meet back in an hour." He looked again at his digital watch. "It's 3:30. Let's meet at the Butterworths' tent at 4:30."

"Is that okay with you, Bill?" Tom asked, not sure he wanted me to agree or disagree.

"No problem, Tom," I smiled. "Except that I don't know if we can carry all the wood we can collect in an hour!" I couldn't resist challenging Edmund.

"Is that so? Maybe we'll just have a little contest to see who can gather the most wood. We'll even give you the advantage of two extra people and still beat you!"

Edmund had to be taught a lesson. His arrogance was getting the best of all of us. "You're on!" I announced, before Tom could attempt to pooh-pooh the idea. "Loser cooks dinner!"

"Deal."

And with that, the Great Firewood Collection Debacle was launched to the horror of Tom, Meg, and Jenny. The rest of us rubbed our hands together in diabolical glee.

There's something about competition that motivates a man like nothing else in the world. The thought of placing a pile of firewood that represents the Butterworths' best efforts next to the meager collection of branches that make up the Holmes contribution was like adrenaline to the body, endorphins to the mind, and caffeine for everything else. It was the ultimate rush.

As Jenny and Meg huddled together to pray for a peaceful resolution to this Battle of the Buddies, it further exemplified how different we are. Women want interaction, men want just action. Women cooperate, men compete. Women want to get together, men use stopwatches to rub out as many stragglers as possible.

It's true, however, that male competition can get terribly out of hand. Edmund's competitive nature, for example, has an outrageous, ugly side to it that I've been aware of for years.

—When I bought a brand new snow shovel down at Pine Woods Hardware, Edmund came home with a snow blower the very next afternoon.

—When I bought a new lawn mower, he had a new riding mower within the week.

—I found a little kiddie pool one year to bail my kids out of the summer heat. Shortly thereafter, Edmund had an above-ground pool that was five feet deep.

—I found a good deal on a small home-stereo system,

Edmund bought a wall full of equipment.

—The year I talked about buying a new car is the year Edmund bought his Lexus.

—The year I sprained my wrist, Edmund broke his arm.

"Let's go, kids!" I yelled now, as I gathered my children around me. Edmund had already done the same thing, as Charlotte and Patti were well on their way to the north side of camp. After prayer with Meg, Jenny jogged to catch up with them.

Once we were out of earshot of the Holmes family, Betsy turned to me, asking, "Do you know what you're doing, Dad?" This question was becoming the choral theme for our summer vacation.

"Usually I don't, but this time I do!" I said in a strategic move that was completely out of character for me. I had a plan.

"The first thing we need to do is borrow the bikes to get back out to the cars," I announced.

"Why?" she asked.

"There's something in the Lexus I need in order to give us a little edge over our competition," I said, purposely creating a sense of mystery.

"An edge?"

"Follow me, boys!" I said, waving my arm forward.

"Dad, please," Betsy implored, still not clear that when I say "boys" I mean her, too.

With me comfortably seated on BJ's handlebars (which now had a pillow draped over them), we rode the dirt road to the Lexus. Jamming my hand down deep into my jeans, I pulled out the key that I'd procured from a naive Jenny. In a second I proceeded to pop the trunk. In the left corner was the backpack I had packed for myself. All of us had backpacks, but of course, the kids' were filled with Walkmans and gum and videos—just in case Tom happened to have a VCR in his motor home.

But my backpack contained something different. It wasn't really a backpack, but a golf bag. As I leaned in to lift it out I felt something in my lower back pull, but I hardly noticed in the raw excitement of the moment. The kids all gathered around me as I unzipped the bag slowly and removed something wrapped in towels. The children's mouths opened in disbelief, then closed to grins of delight as I held up our helper, our advantage, our edge for this contest....

A chainsaw.

"Dad, where did you get this?" Ben asked as he stared at the gleaming steel.

"It's Joe Westman's," I explained, gently patting the saw like it was a newborn baby. "He's a colleague of mine at the community college. A few weeks ago he came into the office bragging about his new purchase of this puppy, so I had a hunch it would come in handy at the camp out. After all, how can you have a camp out without a campfire? I asked if I could borrow it, and he said it was all right."

"Cool!" BJ pronounced.

"It's awesome, Dad!" Bo said, his eyes fixed in a glassy stare at the hardware.

Truly, it was a once-in-a-lifetime sight—their dad holding a power tool. Even I had to admit that. I clucked my tongue, disgusted that I didn't bring my camera along to record this historic moment. Granted, I had no idea how to operate the chainsaw, but it was thrilling enough just to grasp it in my two sweaty hands.

"We've got this contest made in the shade," I said, gazing at my progeny, who by now were all nodding faces filled with exhilarated approval. "It's a done deal."

With that I closed the bag, pushed it to the far corner of the trunk and stood up straight in an effort to shut the trunk lid. It was that straightening up motion that brought with it the pain of a thousand needles, as agony moved from my lower back throughout my entire body.

"Oh, no!" I screamed, as my knees buckled. It looked like I was going to take a tumble, so the kids immediately swung into action...they grabbed the chainsaw as I hit the pavement.

"Everything all right?" Betsy asked.

"Yep—we caught the saw before it hit the ground," Brandon replied, with relief.

"I meant, is everything all right with Dad?" Betsy clarified. The boys looked puzzled.

"I pulled my back," I groaned from my new position on the ground looking up at the dual exhausts of Edmund's Lexus. I had a history of back trouble. It all started by lifting furniture improperly when we moved into our first apartment back in the seventies. I tend to lift with my back, not my legs. That works with copies of dissertations, but not chests of drawers.

To make matters worse, I had always confused the names and densities of certain woods as well. For example, a few years ago when I bent over to lift up a portion of a kitchen nook that I thought was hollow pine, I was surprised to discover it was solid oak. I could feel the muscles in my lower back tear like paper being ripped out of one of those spiral notebooks. As a result, I was in bed for three weeks, eventually limping back to my teaching duties, where I was fodder for a thousand jokes among my students. (I was thirty-five years old, but they saw me all bent over and called me Gramps.)

I healed, but my back would be sensitive for the rest of my life. Today was a perfect example.

"Can you help me up, please?" I squeaked.

BJ and Brandon each offered an arm, which I grabbed onto. Like two typical young men, they constantly competed to see who was stronger. They pulled me up, or more precisely, yanked me up with enough force to send a new ripple of electric shock hurtling through my entire muscular system.

"AAAAHHH!" I winced. Macho Man was shriveling before my very eyes.

"Sorry, Dad," the two boys said in unison.

"I'm all right," I tried to assure five skeptics. "It's just a little strain," I added with as much confidence as a man could while doubled over in indescribable agony. Looking into the disappointed faces of the kids, I realized I better step up the wood cutting plan before all momentum was sadly lost.

"Let's head south and find some wood to chop!" I announced in my leadership role as Captain Bentover. "We'll crank this sucker up and be sitting on a full cord of wood in the time it takes the Holmeses to come up with a couple of sticks!"

The gang appreciated my optimism. Before long we were hiking south, the elderly looking man with the symptoms of osteoporosis in front of a long-legged pretty girl, two young blond boys and last, but not least, two teenage dudes cradling a mechanical treasure like it was the Old Testament ark of the covenant.

Before long we came to a group of six or seven trees that looked to be perfect for our plan. Not only were there small sticks and twigs lying at the base of each tree (perfect for kindling), but there were several branches low enough for us to reach with the chainsaw. It appeared that once again, God was meeting our needs.

"This looks good, kids," I spoke as I waved them to circle around the chainsaw. "Now, if everyone will stand back just a little to give me some working room, I'll crank up our Wonder Saw and begin cutting our victory woodpile!"

The five all took two steps back, excitement returning to their faces at the prospect of beating Charlotte and Patti in a contest of their own design. I, too, mentally envisioned Edmund entombed at the bottom of our woodpile, released only so he could cook us dinner.

"All I have to do is pull this starter-rope-thingy," I muttered to myself as I firmly grasped the black handle attached to the still-white, brand-new starter-rope-thingy. Holding the saw with my left hand, I pulled with my right, and as I did, the pain that shot through my lower back confused me into thinking that the chain-saw was not in my hands anymore, but behind me—and I was leaning on it.

"AAAHHH!" I screamed as all strength left my body. Obviously, starting the saw was going to resemble breaking your leg, then walking to the doctor to tell him about it.

"You okay, Dad?" BJ asked, noticing I was sweating like a Roman fountain.

"Yup," I muttered dishonestly. "I'll try it again. I'll get it started this time, no need to worry."

On this try I dropped the saw to the ground, still unstarted.

"Whoops," I apologized through clenched teeth. "The saw is a little slippery."

"Do you want me to give it a try?" BJ once again asked, still attempting to be helpful.

"No," I pronounced in true male bravado. "I will get this saw running. Just watch."

I held my breath, tightened every muscle in my body, squinted my eyes, and pulled the rope with every ounce of strength I could muster from a body on its last leg (or is it last lower back?). I collapsed to the ground among the twigs and dirt, totally defeated.

Betsy and Brandon gingerly helped me up. They brushed off all the dirt that remained on my Dallas Cowboys T-shirt and then placed me in a seated, upright position under a shady tree nearby. The pain was intense, but the thought of losing the contest was a more agonizing thought.

BJ grabbed the chainsaw. "We won't let you down, Dad!" he yelled triumphantly, as he pulled the cord of the chainsaw over and over, but to no avail.

"Let me try," Brandon offered. He played his version of "Pull the Cord," but his procedure was no more victorious.

"Maybe it needs a woman's touch," Betsy offered hopefully. But the chainsaw was no respecter of gender.

This left Ben and Bo, which in itself was laughable, but Ben bravely took his turn at defeat. Reluctantly he passed the tool to Bo, offering him his first experience with any power greater than an electric toothbrush.

"I'm not as strong as you guys," he said before attempting, so that there would be a valid excuse on the table before his yank of the cord. His first pull caused the engine to turn over with a splendid roar. The six of us cheered. It was the stuff of legend for years to come.

Unfortunately, because of the scream of the saw and the cheers of the kids, no one was aware of the fact that about twenty yards behind us, a California Department of Forestry ranger had pulled up in a faded green jeep.

"You're not planning on cutting anything with that saw, are you?" he asked me calmly.

"Uhhh, hello, officer," I stalled.

"Cutting down trees in a state preserve is against the law, which I am sure you know," he continued.

"Well, of course," I said. It was time to see if I could bluff my way out of this potential sentence of eight-to-ten in the slammer. "Actually, this is a science experiment for one of my kids."

"School's out, isn't it?" he responded.

"It's a summer school project," I continued with my yarn. "We're examining the effect of salt air on a power tool. It was either a chainsaw or an electric screwdriver, and you'd have to agree, an electric screwdriver isn't much of a power tool, so, naturally we thought it would be better if we went with a bigger, more power-ful—"

"Do you really expect me to believe that?" the ranger interrupted.

I hung my head dejectedly. My back hurt intensely, my story wasn't believable, and worst of all, it was 4:25. I only had five minutes left to beat Edmund.

"Okay, officer, you win," I said in defeat, just barely holding back the tears. Placing my two wrists together, I held them up toward him, my back hurting more with each movement. "I'm guilty. Arrest me. Go ahead and cuff me."

"Wait a minute," he said, apparently getting a better look at my face. "Aren't you the friend of the guy I met around here who used to play for the Dodgers and who knows Orel Hersheiser?"

"That's me," I answered, slowly bringing my arms back down to my sides.

He did a 180 on the demeanor meter. "Well, I guess there was no harm done," he concluded, not wanting to jeopardize the offer Tom had made to get him Orel's autograph. Yet he couldn't help looking at me with a mixture of uncertainty and pity. "I can't believe you brought a chainsaw to the beach," he said as he returned to his rusty jeep.

With no time to waste, we picked up some twigs, sticks, and

small branches. As fast as my painful body would carry me, we walked up the beach toward our tent. The Dodger logo set it apart from all others, plus Edmund and his family were already there with a stack of wood. It was clearly bigger than our armfuls of twigs.

The closer we got, the worse I felt, and I'm not talking about my back. Edmund won fair and square and the gloating that would take place would be almost unbearable. I could see the trauma in the faces of my children as they watched Charlotte and Patti skip merrily around the pile of wood that would give them the win.

Only Jenny looked disturbed about the outcome. *My good friend, Jenny,* I thought. *She doesn't want to lose, necessarily, but she needs me in a good mood so I will consider going on this potential blind date with Jessica Quaggenblocker.*

Tom and Meg arrived at the tent at the same time we did. The Butterworths were tired, dirty, sweaty, and in my case, bowed over in pain. But the Grahams always looked like they just emerged from a shower, smelling fresh and clean, hair perfectly in place, clothes just picked up from the dry cleaners.

We dumped our stack next to Edmund's. My mouth opened before his did. "You win, Edmund. Congratulations. On behalf of my whole family, we want to tell you how privileged we feel to be able to cook dinner for you and your family."

"You can stop bowing to me," Edmund mocked, giving the thumbs-up sign to his girls.

"My daddy hurt his back getting his chainsaw out of the trunk of your car!" Bo suddenly screamed out, unwilling to watch his dad take any more abuse.

"Bill, are you all right?" It was Jenny, Meg, and Tom who immediately encircled me, trying to sit me down on the beach.

"Well, Bo's right," I confessed. "I did pull something back there. I've done it before, though. It'll be fine in a few days. Really." I looked up to see the genuine concern on the faces of three very special friends. "Thanks for being so interested," I said, a lump beginning to form in my throat. This was the kind of friendship I was used to.

But then there was Edmund.

"You brought a *chainsaw!*" he exclaimed with enough gusto to blow over the Dodger tent. "Were you gonna *cheat?*"

"Knock it off, Edmund!"

It was Jenny. "You've been giving Bill a hard time ever since we got on the road this morning and I've had just about as much as I can stand. So, if you don't want to finish this vacation alone, you back off. Do I make myself clear, Edmund?"

Edmund stood motionless by the tent.

"I'll cook dinner tonight, if that's okay with everyone," Meg volunteered, once again attempting to distract everyone from the tension that was palpable.

"That's a great idea," Jenny responded. "I'd be very happy to help you, Meg."

"Let's get you back to the Winnebago so you can get off your feet," Tom interjected. All the adults were helpful, except one. Edmund was simmering like a marinara sauce left on low all day. But he dared not let the top off the pot or he would pay dearly—Jenny made that abundantly clear.

It isn't fair! he must have been thinking. He won and he couldn't even gloat. His wife had overridden his exuberance. The thrill of competition had been reduced to an itty-bitty pity party for Mr. Sad Sack Bad Back.

As I hobbled back to the motor home, I pondered about my best friend. Edmund and I had our share of squabbles over the years, but this seemed more intense than any I could remember. *What's wrong with him?* I kept wondering. *Have I done something to offend him?*

The truth was, my back hurt—but fighting with my best friend hurt worse.

Chapter Six

As the sun set on our first day of camping, everyone ooohed and ahhhed about how beautiful it was. For me it was merely another symbol of my disappearing dreams. Macho Camper Man was sinking into the ocean just like the fire-red ball on the western horizon. No one would be impressed with my camping skills now. The darkness of the night might prove to be my ally. At least no one could see how utterly incompetent I was. *Men love darkness, rather than light, for they don't really know how to camp, I dejectedly and silently paraphrased.*

Meg and Jenny had whipped up a dinner in the motor home that was delicious. Even that depressed me, realizing that two women in the comparatively Spartan conditions of a camper could create a meal that was ten times as good as I could cook up in my completely stocked, state-of-the-art, microwave kitchen at home.

We decided to eat under the canopy that extended from the top of the right side of the Winnebago. Tom had already set up one of those laser light bug-zappers to keep away any unwanted dinner guests. The BBBBBUUUUUZZZZZZZAAAAPPPPPPPPP of the light doing its job was our constant companion during our meal. I could imagine toasted bugs piling up, but in order to enjoy my dinner, I never turned around to check.

Jenny had directed BJ and Brandon to a large Coleman cooler that the two of them dragged out from the back of the Winnebago to our awninged, Astro-turfed picnic spot. Upon opening the cooler, they discovered modern-day buried treasure if you're a teenager. Yes, it was filled to the rim with Cokes, Sprites, Dr. Peppers, and Mountain Dews. All seven kids pounced on the new discovery, creating a blur of cans rolling, ice cubes flying, and cold water spraying everywhere.

"There's Diet Coke at the bottom of the cooler," Edmund said to me in a "Fat boys should drink diet" vein.

"Knock it off, Edmund!" Jenny snapped, not wanting this friendship feud to ruin any more of the vacation. "You can drink whatever you want, Bill," she said sweetly in my direction. She spoke so kindly to me, yet when she addressed Edmund she was like a snake squirting venom. Ah, the feminine mystique!

"Jenny and I have already grilled up some beef strips and some chicken strips," Meg announced to all of us. "Over on the picnic table you will find several different Tupperware containers. You can mix together whatever you'd like and call it a fajita!"

As Meg stood there proudly giving instructions, the boys already were pouncing on the picnic table like linebackers on a loose ball. Charlotte, Patti, Betsy, and the adults all watched in horror as the boys violated every table manner known to the civilized world. Between the pushing and tripping, we could hear them lovingly converse with each other:

"Hey, you jerk, I was using the cheese spoon first!"

"That's my tortilla, hog!"

"Pass the olives, oinker!"

"Get your hands off my chicken strips if you ever want to see them again!"

Tom could see how embarrassed I was, so he quickly put a large grin on his face and chimed in, "Well, that's what a picnic should look like, if you ask me! Actually, it reminds me of the time I accidentally walked in on the pregame team meal for the New York Mets!"

Everyone started laughing. You could always count on Tom for the right word at the right time.

After the boys had served themselves, they sat in various folding chairs around the circle, freeing up the picnic table buffet. A casual glance was all that was necessary to see that the neat, orderly dishes of food were now messy, mixed up, tipped over piles of glop.

"Ladies first," Tom proposed, although that was another rule of etiquette already violated by the four gang members I used to call my sons. The ladies smiled but reluctantly walked over to the table to begin the task of resetting the buffet.

"Okay, boys, let's dig in," Tom clapped his hands as he spoke.

Tom made himself two huge fajitas, one beef and one chicken. Edmund did likewise. I grabbed a tortilla, spooned up some beef, added some cheese, tomatoes, and sour cream. I thought carefully about the refried beans, but passed for the good of the group.

Tom, Meg, and Jenny chatted, with Edmund occasionally offering a CPA's stimulating view on issues such as what refried beans really look like when you first open the can, what the temperature really is for mild, medium, and hot salsa, and, of course, the future of guacamole.

I had hoped when dinner was over, I could just toddle off to bed. Wrong. Once dinner had concluded, I found myself wishing it had only just begun. For the next item on the agenda would surely be the ruination of my life.

The campfire roared with Edmund's logs, another painful reminder of defeat in Camperland. We sat as close to the fire as we could, with blankets, quilts, and comforters wrapped around our bodies since summer still brought a chill in the evenings.

Everyone was seated either on driftwood or on blankets right on the beach. Tom brought with him an old guitar from the days when we all had guitars and hair. The word Silvertone across the top assured us that, like so many other teenagers of that generation, we thought we had to have a guitar, and our parents didn't. So the compromise was a visit to Sears, where a Silvertone could be purchased for the price of a clip-on tie. Sure, as teenagers we were embarrassed to have such a cheap guitar, but it was better than no guitar at all. After all, our parents could have bought us an accordion.

As he started to strum, it didn't take long for us to ascertain that Tom only knew three chords. Actually, he knew two well and one poorly. His D and his A were passable, but he couldn't make the G work without muting five of the six strings.

"Let's all sing 'Michael Row the Boat Ashore'!" Tom gushed.

"WHAT?" all the kids asked in unison.

"You don't know that song?" Tom asked incredulously. "Okay, how about 'Lemon Tree'? You know, Trini Lopez?"

The kids were staring at Tom like he was speaking Swahili.

"Do you know any Peter, Paul, and Mary?" he asked, clearly starting to feel out of touch with the circle.

"Aren't they the ones who were puffing the magic dragon, Uncle Tom?" BJ asked. It wasn't clear whether he was sincerely asking or being cynical.

"Actually they claim to this day that the song had nothing to do with drug involvement," Meg interjected, always the one to clear someone's reputation.

"How about 'Blowin' in the Wind'?" Jenny suggested, but she, also, was met with the stare of ignorance.

This stroll down Memory Lane continued for another ten minutes, all to no avail. The kids knew none of the songs that Tom could play with his three chord range...except for one.

Thank God (and orange shag carpet) for "Kum Ba Ya."

We all knew that one, so we sang it heartily. Then we sang it with gusto. Then we sang it again with vigor. Twelve to thirteen times into it, we were singing with quiet reserve, with tenderness, with pianissimo. In other words, we got so tired of it, we all quit, except for Tom. It sounded like Tom Graham, Live at the Campfire.

Meanwhile, it seemed that every time I got settled, the wind would shift, causing the smoke to blow directly into my face. I would bravely choke, cough, and feel my eyes burn until I could take no more. As quietly as possible, I would pick up my chair and move it to another location around the campfire. Sure enough, as soon as I resettled, the wind would shift again.

I noticed that no one else was changing positions. Then again, I really couldn't see anything, since I was a victim of massive smoke inhalation through mouth-hole, nose-holes, and eye-holes.

Even the adults eventually tired of Tom's limited musical range. "How about if we roast marshmallows?" Meg asked, producing a bag of the white, sweet, puffy confections.

The kids all cheered.

"We all need to find a stick to use," Tom instructed.

"The Butterworths brought sticks over here when we were collecting firewood," Edmund said matter-of-factly. Jenny glared at him.

"Edmund," she scolded.

"Well, they did," he protested.

"And I am glad they did," Meg beamed.

"Can someone get me a stick so I can roast a marshmallow?" I asked from my folding chair.

"Here's a good one, Dad," Betsy said, handing me a nice pointy stick.

For a brief moment, it was quintessential camping. The twelve of us, all gathered around the campfire, roasting our twelve marshmallows on twelve sticks. Some knelt by the fire, others sat cross-legged. Still others stood while others squatted.

These were the moments that people referred to when they spoke of positive camping memories. Looking at the faces of my daughter and sons, I realized how selfish I'd been. They really seemed to be enjoying themselves, in spite of my agony. This trip was about family, so maybe I needed to lighten up, maybe I needed to be more positive.

But it was only a brief moment. One by one, we retrieved our marshmallows from the fire. And one by one, we all reached the same conclusion. The marshmallows, once white, puffy, and sweet, were now black, bloated, and tasteless.

What am I missing here? I reflected to myself. *We don't take chocolate bars, unwrap them, and run over them with our cars, do we? We don't take ice cream and set it out in the hot sun to spoil, do we? We don't take red licorice and set it on fire with a lighter, do we? So why do we take a marshmallow and subject it to such a tortuously painful demise?*

It soon became obvious that everyone in our group shared the same feeling. We all participated in the same little scam. We kept a single marshmallow on our stick for the duration of the campfire, while quietly sneaking sweet, unburned marshmallows out of the bag that rested over by Meg's feet.

"Well, I guess it's time to hit the sack," Tom announced, stretching his hands high above his head. "I'm one tired camper."

Soon, the whole circle was yawning, stretching, and winding down after a long day.

"Bill, you're not going to sleep in the tent with your kids, are you?" Meg asked with true concern in her voice.

"You bet I am, Meg. I told my five we were going camping, and by golly, we're going camping. Our tent will be just fine."

"But what about your back?" Jenny asked.

"No problem," I continued to lie. "Actually the best thing for a back in my condition is the firmness the ground will provide." I couldn't believe I was saying that. I needed sleeping on the ground like I needed more smoke in my eyes.

"What a trooper!" Tom exclaimed. Edmund could be heard groaning in the background. Tom, looking from one of us to the other, realized it was time for him to step in and heal this divide once and for all.

"Edmund, Bill, come over here for a second. I want to talk to you two about something."

I painfully got out of my chair and hobbled over to a distant portion of the beach with Tom and Edmund. We were in darkness, but because of the rude noises, I could tell we were on the ice plant.

"Listen, you guys, how about if the three of us get up real early tomorrow and do a little fishing—just us men?"

I couldn't believe what I was hearing.

"Bill, Edmund and I know a little lake about twenty minutes from here that has a great stock of fish. We can sit on a dock, throw out our lines, and relax."

"Gee, Tom, I don't know…" I immediately started to mumble.

"We've brought along everything you need. We have a pole, plenty of bait, and we know a place to stop and get a good strong cup of coffee. They even open at 4 a.m."

"*Four* a.m.?" I asked, swallowing hard.

"Yeah. Of course, we won't get over there till about 4:20, but I know you'll love it!" He sounded so sure of himself. "How does that sound to you, Edmund?"

"It's okay, I guess," Edmund answered.

"Should we tell him what we got for him?" Tom continued on, elbowing Edmund in the ribs.

"I don't care," added the voice of excitement.

"Well," Tom went on wildly, "Edmund and I have these great Hawaiian shirts we wear when we fish. They have flowers and stuff all over them. Mine is white, Edmund's is blue, and we got one for you, Bill!"

"Let me guess," I interrupted. "Is it red?"

"Bingo!" Tom veritably screamed.

Great, I thought to myself, *the American flag goes fishing! This is too much!*

"So, we'll leave at 4:00 and we'll be back right after breakfast. Your kids won't even know you're gone."

Since my kids don't wake up till after lunch, I couldn't argue.

"Are you with us?" he asked, holding his hand up for a high five.

"I guess so," I answered, giving him the best high five I could muster: one in slow motion.

"Great!" Tom was almost frothing at the mouth. "Okay, Edmund, what's the plan?"

"We'll meet at the Winnebagel at 4:00. We'll bike over to the van where we have all the fishing gear. We'll drive to the coffee shop, then to the dock. We should be throwing out our first worm no later than 4:30." Edmund's precision was everywhere, even down to the throwing of the first worm.

With the plan confirmed, we walked back to the campfire. Actually, I should say Edmund walked back, Tom bounded back, and I hobbled back. After the families said good night, the Holmeses and the Grahams left for their campers, leaving the Butterworths alone with their Dodger tent.

Carefully we unzipped the front flap, found our way into the tent, and zipped ourselves in for the night. Six sleeping bags covered the entire floor area. I chose to sleep in the exact middle, the maximum amount of room over my head, so no nasty battles with claustrophobia would develop. The kids surrounded me in their bags.

As we settled down for the night, the kids seemed excited about this adventure of sleeping in a tent. Everyone was exhausted, but no one immediately dozed off. We all laid on our backs in a dark space and quietly chatted with each other.

"Thanks for doing this, Dad," Benjamin said softly. "I know this hasn't been the easiest day for you."

"I agree," Betsy chimed in. "You're making a great effort, Dad."

BJ spoke up. "This reminds me of the night you flooded the house by clogging up all the toilets, Dad. We had no other choice but to sleep in the backyard on blankets and sleeping bags and chaise lounges and lawn chairs."

Everyone started giggling and I chuckled right along, thinking of how rotten I felt that night, but how much I have laughed about it ever since.

"So you guys are having a good time so far?" I asked.

The "yes" was unanimous.

They said good night to each other and soon I was the only one still awake.

This was a wonderful moment, listening to my children

breathe peacefully, but I couldn't help but flash back to the camping trip that had skewed my feelings about the custom forever. I glanced over at BJ, his adult body illustrating to me how much my family has grown over the years. I rolled over and over in my sleeping bag. I was moving all around the tent in my attempt to find a comfortable spot for a night's sleep.

The truth was, I was happy that my family was enjoying themselves, but for the life of me, I could not get comfortable sleeping on the ground inside a giant Dodger bag.

My back was killing me. I gingerly rolled from one position to another, desperately trying to find one position that didn't hurt.

I pulled the sleeping bag up to my chin until I felt too hot. How well did I remember the stories my friends would tell me of the sleeping bags that wouldn't unzip. I had a cousin who spent an entire three-week camping trip in the Colorado Rockies zipped in an old brown sleeping bag from Sears. While everyone else would hike, my cousin would hop. It was embarrassing, of course, but from that trip forward, my cousin had the most well-defined calves and thigh muscles I have ever seen.

Fearing a stuck sleeping-bag zipper, I threw the covers down, but soon felt cold. I missed my pillow, which I had left at home on my bed, of all places. I missed my bed, my wonderful, comfortable, lovable bed.

Now I was not only uncomfortable, I was getting angry. Tom was sleeping in a bed. So was Meg. So were Jenny, Charlotte, and Patti. So was Edmund.

At that last thought I rolled over with an intensity that took me further than I had rolled previously. Being in the middle of the tent, I rolled right into the center post that keeps the tent flying high. I hit that sucker with my entire body weight and it snapped like a toothpick.

The tent immediately collapsed on its six inhabitants, five of which awoke with a start.

"It's nothing to get upset about," I told the kids quickly. They were understandably startled to find the tent lying on them like another layer of blankets. "Everyone just go back to sleep." To my amazement, they did just that.

Which left me flat on my back, holding up the tent with my two arms so it wouldn't fall on the faces of my children. After all, I didn't want them to smother.

I held up the tent for as long as I could. When my arms felt like they were going to explode, I grabbed for the center pole, now in a couple of pieces. I placed each of them at my sides, standing them up. They accomplished the purpose for which I needed them. Granted, from outside the tent now looked like a giant blue sandwich, but the canvas was high enough to allow us to breathe.

I did not sleep for a minute.

Looking back, I guess it was the right kind of evening to have if you had to get up at 3:45.

CHAPTER SEVEN

I guess I did sorta doze off at 3:42.

The portable travel alarm went off at 3:45.

My restful three minutes were over. Immediately I started searching for the alarm. Apparently it was under someone's sleeping bag. When the bell went into its fourth minute of ringing, it occurred to me that this was not going to disturb my children in the least, so I let it scream. I assume it eventually stopped.

Groggy, but awake, I crawled on my belly to place silent kisses on my five kids. Those whose faces were out of their sleeping bags got a kiss square on the cheek. Those completely buried under the covers got a soft pat on the general area that I concluded to be their head. I used Bo's tennis shoes to prop up the broken pieces of the tent's center pole. Once I felt it was secure, I unzipped the two-foot-high low-rider tent. As I gratefully squeezed my way out, I felt like Jonah escaping the great whale, only this rebel wasn't heading to Nineveh, but to find smaller fish to fry.

As I expected, I could stand more upright than I could the night before, but I'd still be looking at more waistlines than faces. I turned to look back at the sorry excuse for a tent. "I'm bent over, the tent's bent over, nothing stands up straight on this trip," I muttered.

I still wore my Cowboys T-shirt and blue jeans. Probably after this fishing experience, I would need to break down and take a shower. I think that is another guy thing, this need to *not* wash the entire time one is on vacation. A real guy doesn't shower, shave, or comb his hair. It's the last throwback to Cave Man times that is still considered politically correct. He can't drag his woman by her hair through the tundra, so he can at least stink (no wonder his woman had to be dragged!).

Walking over to the Winnebago (still with a slight hunch), I realized that I was bringing absolutely nothing with me for a fishing trip. I don't fish, so I have none of the gear. Tom promised me he had a pole, bait, hooks, and bobbers. But really, none of that mattered to me as long as he kept his promise about stopping at the coffee shop.

I don't get the attraction of fishing. You have to deal with all this slimy stuff in order to get ready, and then your reward is a big, stinky, scaly creature that lands on your lap, soiling your clothes and adding to your stress. You sit there in a boat or on a dock or, worse yet, stand in the water with those hip-wader types of boots that make you look half human, half Goodyear tire.

Yet, fishing is clearly a guy thing, so I reluctantly resolved to make the best of it.

"Good morning, Bill!" Tom hissed in a loud stage whisper. He was trying to be excited for me, yet quiet so as to not wake the women.

"Hi, guys," I answered evenly. I didn't try to fake enthusiasm, but rather than sound dejected, I thought the best approach was to come off sounding neutral. I was willing to give this fishing stuff a try. I discovered that it's hard to sound neutral, and I suddenly felt immense respect for everyone living in Switzerland.

"Morning," Edmund replied coldly. He didn't have neutrality

down very well, either. His voice had more of an I-can't-believe-you're-coming-along-to-ruin-our-fishing-trip kind of sound.

Great, I thought, *Edmund is still brooding over something. It's painfully obvious that he doesn't want me here with him, but for the life of me I can't figure out why.*

"Here's your Hawaiian shirt, just like we promised!" Tom announced, handing me a bundle of cloth.

"Thanks," I replied with the sincerity of a seven-year-old boy who receives new underwear from his grandmother for Christmas. It was still so dark, I couldn't see anything. I assumed Tom and Edmund were wearing their Hawaiian attire, so I threw my new shirt over my Dallas Cowboys T-shirt, leaving it unbuttoned for that casual, devil-may-care, fisherman look. This also allowed me to rip it off more quickly if Jessica Quaggenblocker showed up....

Odds were against this, but at the thought I pulled my Dodger cap down low on my face so I wouldn't be recognized in this get-up when the sun came up.

"Everything's all packed and ready in the van," Tom explained. "Let's go!"

I walked toward the bicycles, knowing that we had a little two-wheel journey before we met up with our four-wheeled friend. Tom saw where I was headed and grabbed me by the shoulder. "The bikes won't be necessary, buddy," he said.

"Why not?" I asked.

"Because our friend, Edmund, has already been up for an hour. He rode a bike out to the van and drove it back over by the entrance. So we can walk over to the front gate where our chariot awaits!"

"Gee, thanks, Edmund," I said, somewhat stunned that he would do something so gracious knowing full well that it would benefit me.

"No problem," he answered flatly. "We couldn't leave the bikes out there while we fished, so I thought this would be easier for everyone." His explanation made sense. So much about Edmund made sense. He was usually a clear-thinking, conscientious, law-abiding man who was wonderful to have as a best friend. It was only since this trip began that he'd become Official Burr Under My Saddle.

For a split second, our glances met and there was a look of the old friendship that had characterized our relationship for so many years. But we both quickly looked away.

Walking out the main gate, we met our friend the ranger. He was still so impressed that Tom had played with the Dodgers, he virtually ignored Edmund and me.

"Oh, that's your van by the gate," the ranger said in a surprised and somewhat embarrassed tone. "Well, just a second, let me get that ticket out from under your windshield wiper." He was already out of his post, heading toward the front of the van. "My mistake. I thought this van belonged to someone else. There's no problem with your parking here for a few minutes, Mr. Graham."

He ripped the ticket into a dozen pieces. I was waiting for him to eat it.

"Thanks, friend," Tom smiled.

"It's just fine," the ranger replied. "I'll just circle around on the CB and cancel that tow truck."

"I appreciate it," Tom continued.

"You guys have a great day now, y'hear?"

"We'll do it!"

And with that, we climbed into the van, Tom in the driver's seat, Edmund up front with him, and me in the back (no Barbies back there—I checked). Heading east out of the campgrounds, it was easy to notice that the roads were empty. No one, I repeat, *no one* was up this early for any reason (with the exception of the tow truck, which we passed on our way out). "Are we gonna stop for coffee?" I asked, the only important issue in my mind.

"You can count on it," Tom replied. "We'll stop up the road here a bit. Besides having the best coffee in town, this place sells the best fresh bait!" In an instant reflex I imagined earthworms swimming around merrily in my large coffee mug.

"Worms?" I said, disgust in my voice.

"Yes, they sell worms there," Tom replied. "However, Edmund and I have had better luck with those little minnows. The bass really go for those babies, isn't that so, Edmund?"

"Yes it is," Edmund replied. Poor Tom. He was trying so hard to bring Edmund and me back into the our warm, friendly teepee. But Edmund can be one stubborn cuss, and his streak was showing.

We drove further down the highway, Tom commenting on a billboard or a street sign every now and then. But mostly we drove in silence. Between tension and fatigue, there wasn't a lot to say. Granted, I imagine a van full of women would have figured a way around this. But we three men had nothing to say, and that about says it all.

Eventually, our van chugged down a desolate street to a lone building that was lit up like a beacon. As we got closer, a hand-painted sign declared: *Denise's Coffee Shop*. In small print underneath it read: *Fresh Coffee and Fresh Bait*.

When our van doors opened, three semicomatose men in desperate need of caffeine shuffled out into the crisp morning air. I blindly followed Edmund, who blindly followed Tom, who opened the front door, causing a sleigh bell to ring overhead. The bell frightened me, so I jumped with a start, instantly reminding myself that my back still hurt.

"It's okay," Edmund calmed me, forgetting that we were feuding.

Now, for the first time since rising, we were under enough light to see what we looked like. It was just as Tom had described. He was in a Hawaiian shirt of a white base with colored flowers and palm trees all over it. Edmund was in a blue version and I looked down to see that in my red floral shirt, I perfectly rounded out the total look of Our American Flag Goes to Hawaii.

"Good Morning, Denise!" Tom said.

"Well, hush my mouth, if it isn't Tom Graham!" Denise replied with a drawl that told me she wasn't born and raised in central California. Maybe central Tennessee was a better guess. She was middle-aged, with striking blonde hair and pretty blue eyes, and dressed in a red and black flannel shirt and jeans. Her look and her accent were exactly like Ellie May's from the old television show, *The Beverly Hillbillies*. Granny and Jethro, however, were nowhere to be found.

"It's good to see you again, Denise," Tom reached over and shook her hand like he was running for mayor from these here parts.

"Who's y'alls friends?" she asked, pointing her finger at Edmund and me.

"Oh, forgive my manners," Tom said apologetically. "This is Edmund Holmes, whom you've met before, actually. And this is our good friend, Bill Butterworth. He and his family are joining us for a camp out over at Happy Clam. We guys are sneaking out for some fishing."

"Well hey, Edmund, hey, Bill," she answered back with a smile that was as contagious as the mumps. Before long, we were all smiling back at her, although Edmund looked a little hurt that Denise hadn't remembered him from before.

"Let's start out with three jumbo coffees," Tom said as he scratched his chin in a real look of concentration. "Edmund, how much bait should we get?"

"You best get a bunch," Denise answered on Edmund's behalf. "Just lookin' at y'uns convinces me that y'all will be reelin' 'em in as fast as you can bait your hooks. You best be prepared."

With typical male ego firmly in position, we gullibly bought every line pretty Denise would send our way—and enough bait to stock a commercial fishing boat for a year.

"Don't forget our thermoses," Tom added, producing two large bottles that would hold enough coffee to get most people through the week, but would only do us for three hours.

We gathered our purchases, paid Denise, bid her our fond farewells. I didn't know whether to say "Good-bye," "Aloha," or "Y'all come back now, y'hear?"

Back in the van, it was a very short drive to Lake Gomez. Tom knew exactly where he was going, and we were parked by the dock in a matter of minutes. My two compadres were already unloading the gear. I wanted to help but figured the best thing I could do was sit alone in the van, nursing my coffee.

Tom saw things differently.

"Come on, Bill! We need your help here! Grab that red tackle box over there," he ordered, pointing to a rectangular tin box over by the pile of rods. It looked like a tool box to me, but then again, I don't know much about that either.

We walked the short distance to the dock and continued on its rickety wood planks to the end that jutted out over the lake. It was still quite dark, the sun not due for another hour. Tom's lantern led the way as we walked by faith, not by sight, on this dock that had "Built in 1810" written all over it.

Tom and Edmund placed their paraphernalia strategically

around them like seasoned fishermen would. It was clear they wanted to keep me away from anything that demanded knowledge of this craft. Or, put another way, they didn't want me to hurt myself.

Without too much effort, my two fellow travelers were now sitting on the edge of the dock with their legs dangling halfway to the water. The lake was black, except for the reflections created by the lanterns and the moon.

"Sit down with us here, buddy," Tom offered invitingly. With Edmund hugging the right side of the dock and Tom comfortable on the left, I tried to plop down in between them, but when a sharp bolt of pain shot up my back, I slipped. I managed to catch myself from falling into the lake, but I scraped my hand on the dock in the process.

"Oww!" I whimpered as I brought my hand up with three or four tiny spears of wood attached. It looked like I was into acupuncture with toothpicks.

"Watch out for splinters," Edmund said, a smirk just barely visible in the lantern's glow.

I yanked the splinters from the palm and little finger of my right hand and put the bloody paw in my mouth to wash away the blood. But as soon as I would take my hand out of my mouth, I could feel the trickle of something wet rolling down past my hand to my forearm before dripping into the water.

"There aren't any sharks in this lake, are there?" I asked Tom nervously. I had visions of Jaws rising up out of the water to swallow up Splinter Boy.

"Not this lake or any other lake, you Twinkie," Edmund retorted. "Sharks are found in the ocean, in salt water."

"I knew that," I barked back the way a four-year-old does when he has no idea what he is talking about.

"Let's bait our hooks and pull in some of those bass!" Tom bellowed in his constant effort to keep Edmund and me from our ongoing argument.

Tom and Edmund joyously plunged their hands into the bait bucket, each grabbing a slippery little minnow and impaling it on the end of their fish hook. In the blink of an eye, they had both cast their lines to perfection, a red and white bobber barely visible in the predawn gray. The only sounds were the occasional winding of the reel and the slurps and "ahhhs" men make when they sip coffee.

By this time it was obvious that everyone was fishing except me. I turned to my left, swallowing hard as I observed the rod and reel that Tom had carried out for me. I picked it up; it felt lighter than I thought. Edmund had been watching me, so once I had the rod in hand, he gleefully stuck the bait bucket under my nose. The smell was nauseating to a city kid who had only seen fish in aquariums.

"Stick your hand in there and pick a nice juicy minnow!" Edmund said with a certain degree of relish in his voice (relish in his voice…is it possible to have mustard in your voice? or ketchup in your voice? Just a passing thought).

"All right," I answered. But it took longer to grasp one of those slimy varmints than I thought it would. They felt like little wiggly globs of grease, and as much as I wanted to grab one—I didn't want to grab one. Finally, I clenched a minnow, pulling it out of the bucket with a large sigh of relief and a sense of great accomplishment.

"Okay. Now stick it on your hook." Edmund's instructions were blunt, no feelings spared.

"You mean I have to stab the minnow?" I repeated, the full impact of this concept finally dawning on me. "The minnow will die…" I said, my voice trailing off into the lake's dark surface.

"Oh brother!" Edmund scoffed. Turning to Tom, he added, "I told you he couldn't do it. I told you it was a mistake to bring him out here with us. He's more concerned with the life expectancy of bait than he is with catching any bass!"

"No, I'm not!" I shouted. Defiantly I pushed that minnow firmly onto my hook. Actually I pushed that minnow so firmly onto my hook that in a split second, the hook was embedded deeply in my thumb. "OHH NUTS!!" I cried painfully. The shock caused me to stiffen up, reminding me that my back was still gimpy as well.

Tom and Edmund reached over to help me, but I would have none of it. In my awkward position on the dock, all I had left was my pain and my pride. Stubbornly, I yanked the hook out of my thumb, taking what felt like about three-quarters of my thumb with it. I watched as the blood from the top of my hand merged with the blood still oozing from the bottom of my hand in crimson union. I was suddenly glad that I was chosen to wear the Hawaiian shirt that was red.

"Let me take a look at that hand," Tom said soothingly, reminding me of the camp counselor I had one summer who wanted to examine my archery accident.

"Ah, don't worry about it," I replied, burying my bloody right hand under my left hand. "It's only a flesh wound."

Tom and Edmund both turned to stare at me.

"Are you sure you're okay?" Tom persisted.

"I never felt better," I answered. By now I was sitting on my right hand, attempting a tourniquet effect by cutting off the blood to my hand by pressing down on my wrist with my right buttock. This is not easy with a bum back.

"LET'S FISH!" I said emphatically, desperately trying to turn the spotlight away from my new role as Bloody Boy the Fishing Fool. I was actually longing to be back in the collapsed tent with my five children. I threw forward my newly baited fishing line. It sounded like an excellent cast, but alas, the bobber was only four feet in front of the dock, the ripples on the lake embarrassingly close to shore.

"Need some help?" Edmund asked.

"Not from you."

"Fine."

"Fine."

So the three of us sat in silence, legs swaying off the side of the dock, coffee by our sides, and absolutely motionless lines. I was utterly overcome with boredom. Fortunately, the Lord knew of my plight, so he allowed our attention to be drawn to the other side of the lake as we watched a bright red ball of fire come up over the east, announcing to all that it was going to be a scorcher today. *It'll be cooler back at the beach*, I reminded myself.

The silence was rudely interrupted by a sudden yank on Edmund's line. "Whoa Nellie!" he giggled as he began reeling in his catch. "This is a big one, guys!" Edmund enjoyed doing his own play by play. "I've got to be real careful, 'cause I don't want to lose this baby." He gave his rod and reel his full concentration. "Steady...steady...here we go.... Oh, this is a beauty, guys!"

Sure enough, at the end of Edmund's line was one fine bass. Not being a fisherman, I am hard pressed to give specifications, but let's call it three feet long and one hundred pounds—give or take an ounce or two. (There are certain traits of fishermen that I can pick up quickly.)

"Way to go, Edmund!" I cheered, genuinely pleased that this catch made my friend so happy. He smiled, nodded at us, and the three of us rejoiced.

Placing the fish in an empty white bucket which he pulled close to his side of the dock, Edmund smiled as if he had just won the lottery. Once again, he baited his hook and did his best to cast his line close to his original spot.

"Congratulations, Edmund!" Tom applauded. "Isn't that great, Bill?" he elbowed me in the left rib cage.

"I'm thrilled," I replied. I really meant it, too, but apparently it wasn't convincing to Edmund.

"At least I caught something," he responded defensively. "Your minnow is probably swimming around the lake free as a bird. And no fish is interested in the part of your thumb that's hanging off the hook."

I glared at Edmund. Everything he said was probably true, but nonetheless, it hurt. "Edmund, why don't you just jam a sock in your—" I never got to finish my statement as my pole suddenly bent over with such tension that it looked like the arc of a rainbow.

"Bill's got himself a fish!" Tom beamed with satisfaction. "Take it easy with her now."

Having never been bass fishing, I had no idea if I was taking it easy or taking it hard. I just started reeling in my line as fast as I could. Whatever was on the other end was certainly heavy! I was sweating, dark spots forming on my blood-red Hawaiian shirt. Out of the corner of my eye, I observed that Edmund's jaw was dropped so far that he looked ready for his semiannual teeth cleaning.

"Steady as she goes," Tom kept counseling.

Was I looking unsteady?

"How much more line is out there in the water?" I asked between huffing and puffing.

"Just a little bit further and you'll have her," Tom smiled.

He was right. About fifteen seconds later a fish ascended out of the water bigger than anything I had ever seen north of Sea World in San Diego. It was a bass the size of Brazil.

Okay, maybe it wasn't the size of Brazil, but as clear as the bugged eyes of this fish—it was way bigger than Edmund's!

That's all that really mattered.

And it was more than Edmund could take. "Why should you catch the biggest fish?" he suddenly screamed, his voice causing Tom and me to jump in startled surprise. "You don't even know how to fish and here you go catching the big one…it's not fair!"

"No one ever said life was going to be fair," I replied in the tone I used to lecture my sons.

And that's when it happened.

"If I wasn't a fine, upstanding Christian gentleman, I would come over there and slug you right now!"

"Oh yeah, right," I said, adding a time-tested line from my childhood, "you and whose army?"

Edmund stood up and lurched toward me in a macho-fake gesture that guys use when they don't really want to fight but feel it's unmanly to ignore the verbal jabs.

Right then, as he lurched forward, he tripped on the bait bucket, fell hard into me, and launched me into the lake.

Still holding on to my big bass, I sunk to the bottom like a stone. Frantic, my life flashing before my eyes, I flailed at the water, still unwilling to release the fish. But the lake revived my big catch, who started wiggling and slapping me with his tail. In a millisecond that I knew I would regret the rest of my life, I loosened my grip and the fish swam to freedom, with not so much as a fin flip for good-bye.

I resurfaced to the sight of Tom stripping down to his Dodger boxer shorts, preparing for a Voyage to the Bottom of the Sea.

Edmund, looking sheepish, was gathering his belongings. Tom extended the right hand of fellowship, which I gladly accepted, and he pulled me back up to the dock.

Not only was I still bleeding, but I was now drenched and covered with a green, slimy kind of dirt that one can only find at the bottom of a lake. My tan Dodger cap had fallen off in the confusion, finding a new home somewhere on Lake Gomez. I ran my hand back through my hair and the result, I was told later, was a reddish green blond color which stood straight up thanks to algae shampoo and seaweed conditioner.

We rode the van back to the Happy Clam Campground in absolute silence. Edmund was furious, I was furious, and Tom was just about at the point of giving up. Most painful of all, I was fuming over the fact that I now had to join the ranks of just about every other fisherman I had ever met. Now I, too, had a whopper of a story about the big one that got away.

And, of course, no one would ever believe it.

By the time we arrived back at camp, I smelled ripe. I was still bent over with a bad back, crusty blood covered my right hand, my clothes were sopping wet, muddy, and stinking of rancid lake water. My hair had stiffened up to a five-inch-high reddish green lawn, in desperate need of mowing.

So, it was not exactly the perfect timing for Jenny's announcement when we stumbled back to the Winnebago: "Hi, Bill! I'd like you to meet Jessica Quaggenblocker...."

CHAPTER EIGHT

I t was juxtaposition personified. Here was a woman of radiant beauty with the world's ugliest name. Jessica Quaggenblocker was a tall, slender, tan woman of forty with striking blue eyes, blonde hair, and a great smile.

Her choice of clothing was simply divine, but I'll spare you the details.

Then there was me. When Jenny introduced us, I automatically offered my right hand—which screamed for an emergency room.

But this was just the tip of the iceberg we call ugly. I was covered, head to toe, with dried blood, dried green slime, and dried silt from the bottom of the lake. I looked like a salad in a Halloween Health Food Store.

Plus I stunk. After a few quick calculations, I concluded that Jessica was downwind from me, sealing my doom.

"It's nice to meet you," Jessica said. Her smile was warm enough, but I winced as she said the N-word. "It's *nice* to meet you." Now I knew for sure this was going nowhere. When a person says it is "nice" to meet you, what he or she really means is,

"You're not at all what I thought you would be, so if we could make this a brief introduction, I'd be grateful."

But in my case, who could blame her?

It did not escape my glance that Edmund went out of his way to give Jessica a friendly hug, a peck on the cheek, and, most annoyingly, a rather lengthy secret in her ear. My blood boiled as I watched him whisper to her. As he did this, she turned my way several times, holding back laughter. It wasn't enough that Edmund had knocked me into a lake and lost my first fish, now he was bombing my efforts at dating a wonderful lady. This was war.

"Hey, Dad!" BJ greeted me. "What in the world happened to you?" he added as he looked me up and down.

"Hrrrumphh," I replied wearily.

"Were you guys caught in a mud slide?" he asked, excitement in his voice. The thought of his dad flirting with danger was far-fetched, but appealing.

"There was a little…accident," Tom responded, once again playing the role of peacemaker, "but everyone is safe and sound now."

I was about to object to the veracity of the phrase "safe and sound," when the rest of my kids appeared from the Winnebago. "Hooray, Daddy's back! Now we can go rent the Funcycles on the beach! This is gonna be a real kick, Dad! You'll love it!"

I have learned that when my children feel the need to convince me of the fun I am going to have in advance of the event in question, this means not only that I won't have fun, but my very life is probably in danger.

"Bill, I've invited Jessica to ride the Funcycles with us on the beach today," Jenny added, smiling a contented grin. All that was missing was the song "Matchmaker" from *Fiddler on the Roof* playing in the background.

I smiled a happy smile but instantly sensed that I had algae on a few of my teeth. Less than sexy. Less than desirable.

"Yes, I'm looking forward to our biking excursion!" Jessica distorted the truth most beautifully. Beneath my mud exterior, I was filled with warm feelings...feelings I hadn't felt in a real long time.

"Dad, why do Uncle Edmund and Uncle Tom look all clean but you look like you had a mud bath?" Brandon asked.

The only answer I could think of was the one all parents use when they either don't know the answer or don't want to deal with it right now. "I'll tell you when you're older," I muttered.

Meg broke in. "We have the Funcycles reserved for an hour and a half," she announced, glancing down at her watch. "And actually, we need to scurry down there right away, because our time starts in about ten minutes. If we're late, they'll give the bikes to someone else."

"No time for a shower?" I asked, half kidding, thinking she wouldn't hold me to the ten-minute rule.

"I'm afraid that's correct, Bill. Maybe you can just change into some clean clothes, but even that will have to be quick."

I just stood there motionless, not believing what I was hearing. "Look at me!" I wanted to shout. "How can I possibly impress this incredibly beautiful woman if I look like the jungle and smell like the sewer?" I knew my impression of Swamp Thing was getting me nowhere.

As if on cue, Edmund interjected: "Oh, by the way, Tom, we need to empty those tanks in the Winnebagel when we get back from the beach. I'm not sure how full the gray water tank is, but I know the sewage tank is close to overflowing."

"Thank you for sharing that warm fuzzy thought, Edmund," I said, looking over at Jessica with a "he's not with me" expression.

I shed the aloha look by ripping off the muddy gift from Tom and Edmund, leaving me in the gray Dallas Cowboy T-shirt I'd been wearing since we left home. Home…it seemed light years away. A warm shower, soap, shampoo, an oversized towel, and a clean pair of boxers would have to stay a fantasy for now, along with the hope that I'd be impressive at all to Jessica Quaggen-blocker, former Miss Orange County.

"So, Jenny tells me that you used to be Miss Orange County," I stammered, trying to start a conversation while walking down to the booth on the beach that rented the bikes.

Jessica threw her perfectly blonde head back and laughed perfectly. "Oh, that Jenny!" she giggled, slapping her thigh as she said it, "she tells everybody that story. I'll venture that she pointed out that Michelle Pfeiffer was a former Miss Orange County, too."

"It's a story? Like a pretend, made-up story?" I inquired, coming back to the first part of her statement.

"That's right," she replied.

"You were never Miss Orange County?"

"No, I was never Miss Orange County." She turned and looked at me, "Does that bother you?"

"Well, no…not really…it's no big deal." I was rambling like a toddler. "How did the story get started?" I asked, feeling an immense need to put the speaking spotlight back on her.

"When I met Jenny, we were working at a bank together down in Mission Viejo, which is in south Orange County. Anyway, I was chosen as the Queen of the bank one year, which is what Jenny refers to. The truth is I was never chosen Miss Orange County, but I was chosen Miss Orange County Savings and Loan in 1975!"

She laughed again and I joined her. We walked a little further in silence. *She sure looks like a beauty queen to me!* I thought. *Who cares whether she was Miss Orange County or not? It's what's inside that counts anyway. She really is beautiful. Plus, who am I to be so picky about all the details of her life, walking along the beach here like a hobo in search of a Dumpster?*

"I just want you to know that I really appreciate your coming out here today." I turned and looked at her as she continued to smile sweetly at me.

"Well I'm thrilled that Edmund and Jenny invited me," she responded sincerely.

"Yeah, but I mean with me looking so gross and everything, I really appreciate that you didn't cut out as soon as you saw me."

"I wouldn't do something like that to such a nice man," she answered as I blushed.

"That's nice of you to say," I said sheepishly.

"When my marriage ended I thought my world was over," she said softly. "I felt the rejection so strongly that I wondered if I would ever get on with my life."

"I know the feeling," I interjected.

"I know you do, Bill, because Edmund and Jenny told me all about you. That's why I can call you such a nice man, because your friends think so highly of you."

I was just about to cry, I was so choked up.

"I wouldn't have missed today for anything," she concluded.

Shortly we were at the appointed place at the appointed time. A sign that read *Frankie's Funcycles* greeted us as an overweight man in a tiny T-shirt nodded his welcome to our party.

"We're the Graham group," Meg took charge, stepping forward to the counter.

"Ah yes," Frankie said, looking down at his tattered appointment book. "The lucky party that wants thirteen bikes!"

"You're the lucky one," I said to him under my breath. "Thirteen bikes times eight bucks per bike equals a big profit margin for Frankie-boy."

"Let's see how much you owe me," he gloated.

"One hundred and four dollars," Edmund answered, displaying his incredible grasp of multiplication.

"Just a second, just a second," Frankie scolded, determined to get his little pocket calculator to work. This was one classy businessman. Not only was he dressed like a carnival worker, he was using a calculator he got as a free gift for subscribing to *Beach Bike Monthly*.

"This is gonna be great, Dad!" Ben kept up the children's tag-team effort to keep me encouraged about this adventure. I smiled at Ben with a smile that looked like I needed more fiber.

"So we need six adult bikes and seven kids' bikes, right?" Frankie asked, scoping out the entourage.

"No, I need an adult bike," Brandon answered in a heartbeat. He was sixteen. No more child prices, this guy was a full-fledged adult. "When I was a child I understood as a child, but when I became sixteen, I wanted nothing more to do with child price breaks."

"I need an adult bike, too," BJ echoed.

"Me, too," Betsy added.

"That's nine adult bikes and four kids, right?" Frankie was growing impatient, the $104 apparently burning a hole in his pocket.

"That will be just fine," Tom answered. And with that, we were given our respective vehicles and pointed in the direction of the beach.

"Don't forget, be back in an hour and a half," Frankie yelled from his dune buggy as he drove off to enjoy the spoils of his victory.

A Funcycle is one of those three-wheeled bikes especially designed for riding on the beach. It's built long and low to the ground, like a banana, allowing the person riding to pedal more effectively on the sand. It didn't take too long to realize that the wet sand down by the ocean was the place to be. The dry sand was more difficult and we wanted fun, not challenge.

"All right, Dad!" my kids cheered in unison as I pedaled my machine with a newfound energy out to the lead spot in front of the pack. It looked like it was going to be difficult, but it was actually pretty easy. At least this is how I felt for the first two minutes I was pedaling.

I confess, I had several agendas operating at this point. First, this appeared to be an excellent way to spend time with my kids. Second, by riding out in front, I could zigzag my machine to blow sand in Edmund's face. And third, not the least of all, was that by riding boldly, strongly, in he-man fashion, I was going to impress Jessica Quaggenblocker, whom I decided I was smitten with. Nobody had looked forward to being with me for years and I wasn't going to let an opportunity to impress her go by. She seemed to enjoy my antics, too, for her contagious laugh filled the ocean air.

As my Funcycle picked up speed I drove perilously close to the ocean. Once in a while the mist of the ocean sprayed me with a cooling drizzle that not only refreshed, but also cleaned me up a bit. I stopped and uncharacteristically pulled off my Dallas Cowboy t-shirt, revealing the whitest chest God ever created.

There is a reason why middle-aged men keep their T-shirts on. Gravity. I was no Mr. Buff who could turn protein into steel. I was more like a scientist who turned vanilla ice cream into Jell-o. I was translucent white—and I jiggled.

As I rode on, I was so into the exhilaration of this experience, I threw my head back, just like Eric Liddell did in *Chariots of Fire* when he sprinted on the beach. Granted, he was gracefully running, and I was crazily pedaling, but it felt the same to me. We both just wanted to feel God's pleasure.

However, I should also add that Eric Liddell had the long, sleek body of a runner, whereas I had breasts—and a very bad back.

I was completely in a world of my own, oblivious to all else—including how *slowly* I was actually going—when the jumbo aspirin I'd taken before we left suddenly wore off. As my back began to scream in protest, I woke up and realized I was not only no longer ahead of the pack, I'd fallen so far behind that my family and friends were nowhere in sight.

I glanced at my watch. "We have to be back at Frankie's in twenty minutes!" I shouted to no one in particular. "So where did everybody go?"

I spun around on my tricycle and began pedaling home. To the best of my recollection, it took me about twenty-three seconds of pedaling home to realize why the trip down the beach had been so effortless. I'd been riding with the wind behind me.

Now the wind howled in my face, and the hot sun glared down on my broken back. My thighs screamed. My lungs burned. The once-refreshing ocean mist blasted sand into my eyes and inside my mouth and nose. Rather than enjoying the ocean, I was frantically searching for lifeguard stands in the eventual likelihood that I would need paramedical attention.

The pedaling became so painful, I lost all moisture in my mouth. Apparently, it was relocating to my eyeballs, for large alligator tears started rolling down my cheeks, silent testimonies to a life of suffering. Looking at my watch, I calculated I had ten minutes to get back to the spot that had taken me over an hour to pedal from with the wind. Then, God supernaturally intervened.

Did he lift up my Funcycle, delivering me back to Frankie's Funcycle stand on the wings of angels?

No.

Did he empower my legs with superhuman strength, allowing me to mount up with wings like eagles?

No.

Did he miraculously place my bike on the water, causing it to glide effortlessly on the surface, just as Christ had walked on the water?

No.

I said God intervened, but I didn't necessarily mean that it was a positive intervention. For, as I pedaled along in utter despair and painful agony, just as I had adjusted to the idea of ending up the Hunchback of Notre Dame, for no apparent reason, the Lord himself took hold of my Funcycle and the chain inexplicably left its position connecting the pedals with the wheels.

It was already time to be back, and here I was stuck on the beach with seemingly miles to go and no effective means of transportation. I rolled off the bike, stumbling onto the sand. Picking myself up and brushing off, I turned my attention to the errant bike chain. Silently I applauded myself that at least I knew where it belonged, but alas, I had no clue how to get it there.

"Let's try this," I mumbled, as I grabbed the chain in my right hand and attempted to line it up with the round, saw blade looking disc with the teeth. The chain was just a smidge too small to fit around the disc easily. And for me, if it didn't go on easily, it wasn't going on.

Dropping the chain in defeated disgust, I observed that I now had black grease all over my hands and forearms, and even small stripes appeared on my polar-bear-like stomach. Now I had a zebra thing going.

Seriously ticked off, I kicked the front tire with every ounce of strength I could muster from a leg that was still trembling from more pedaling than I had done in over twenty years. Needless to say, I caused no damage.

By the time I got back to Frankie's Funcycle stand, it was over an hour later than the agreed-upon return time. Frankie, knowing the value of repeat customers, proceeded to cuss me out with words that I hadn't heard since I accidentally mowed down my neighbor's prize vegetable garden with my weed-whacker gone amok.

"Where are the rest of the folks in my party?" I asked weakly, once Frankie had exhausted the swearing spectrum.

"They turned in their bikes a long time ago," he said. "They waited around awhile, but the accountant guy said you'd be gone the rest of the day. He said when they followed the trail to come back here, you probably just kept pedaling down the beach like an idiot."

"Edmund," I muttered. "That skunk."

"If you don't mind me saying, you're the one that looks like the skunk," Frankie laughed derisively at my black grease on snow-white skin. I wished I were a skunk so I could have sprayed him. *See you in a bath of tomato juice!* I thought to myself.

"That'll be another twenty-five bucks to fix the chain, and then we'll call it even." Frankie, he of no cooth (is that coothless?), was charging me extra for giving me an inferior bike!

"No, I don't think so, pal," I responded, trying to sound as tough as I could.

"Fraid so, buddy-boy," he argued. "The bike broke while in your possession, so you gotta pay up!"

"But I didn't break it!" I pleaded.

"Then who did?" he asked.

I thought for a moment, then tried my luck. "It was an act of God," I answered in total sincerity.

"Yeah, sure, pal. God broke the bike, but spared you. You gotta be kiddin' me." His lip curled up as he laughed the laugh of a man who had smoked enough cigarettes to burn down Honduras. "Life's unfair, but it ain't that unfair!"

I threw down his money and hobbled back to camp. On the way, I was reminded of another reason why I don't usually take my shirt off. I was now sunburned to a crisp.

"Dad's back, everyone!" Betsy yelled in relieved tones. "What happened to you? We were all worried about you!"

"Not everyone was worried," I barked, upon seeing Edmund emerge from his tent trailer. "Anyway, my bike broke," I started my tirade. "The chain fell off, so I had to walk it back, and the wind was blowing and I thought I was gonna die, but God spared me so that I can be here with my family to make a memory."

The drama was thick enough to cut with a knife.

"Are you all right, Bill?" Jenny asked in genuine concern.

"Yeah. Fine."

"That's good," Jenny responded.

I paused for a moment, looked around the campsite, then asked, "Jenny, where's Jessica?"

"She had to go back already, so she wanted me to tell you good-bye and that she really enjoyed meeting you."

"Did she say anything else?" I asked, hopefully.

"Well, yes," Jenny flashed a sly smile, "she did say that she thought you were nice."

I winced. It was turning out to be that kind of day.

Chapter Nine

ot too long after my arrival back at a Jessica Quaggenblocker-
less camp, I could have sworn that Edmund and Tom were
packing up to leave, too.

Edmund was moving all the bicycles leaning up against
the motor home, while Tom was carefully breaking down the
Winnebago's awning. I'm not much of a camper, but even I knew
this looked suspicious.

*They're both sick and tired of having to deal with me, I thought in
a superior case of self-pity. I've pushed them both too far. Edmund is
mad as a hornet at me for some unknown reason, and Tom is exhausted
with trying to referee our fight. But I can't believe they would pull up
stakes (no pun intended) and leave town. They're really punishing their
families by doing this.*

Then it hit me. *Maybe just the two of them are leaving! That's their
revenge! They're leaving me with the women and girls…the only adult
male, sailing adrift in a tiny rubber life raft on a tempestuous sea of
feminine waters. Random curlers float by, as well as mascara, mousse,
and fingernail polish in some womanly color the label calls Parisian
Pink… .*

I was close to having a panic attack at the very thought of my two best friends leaving me alone to vacation with the Campfire Girls. Then it hit me. Actually, the girls had been quite kind to me...maybe it wouldn't be so bad after all!

"So, what are you two doing?" I blurted out.

"We're leaving you," Edmund answered, his back to me as he continued to systematically move the bikes to their new spot up against the tent trailer.

"Ah ha!" I retorted, clearly sounding the call that I knew this was their plan. "Well, if I were you two, I would give some serious consideration to your decision."

Edmund looked over at Tom. They both exploded into fits of raucous laughter that was so loud, people from other campers were climbing out of their aluminum shells like turtles to see what the ruckus was all about.

"Why are you laughing?" I demanded.

"You are such a yutz, Butterworth!" Edmund finally replied.

"We're not leaving you, buddy," Tom chimed in.

"Then why are you breaking down the awning and restacking the bikes and folding up the chairs?" I sounded like a hurt puppy.

"We're emptying the tanks in the Winnebagel, you wing nut!" Edmund said. It was painful to be called a wing nut by someone who insisted on calling the motor home a Winnebagel, but I bit my tongue.

"He's right, Bill," Tom added. "You see, when the gray water tank and the sewage tank get full, we have to drive over to a central site in order to empty our tanks."

"What a hassle," I commented. Edmund threw an angry look my way, then barked, "You're hassled? Tom and I are doing all the work, and you say that you're hassled?"

"I'm sorry," I replied, realizing Edmund had a point. "What can I do to help?"

"Well, I think we've just about got it handled," Tom answered.

"Perfect timing, as usual," Edmund muttered.

"Jump in with us, Bill," Tom offered kindly. "We'll give you a little clinic on the proper emptying of waste tanks."

Meg and Jenny offered to oversee the cleanup of all the children while we were off to the Dump. They were lining up seven sons and daughters in preparation for their march to the public showers, located about a quarter of a mile away, over by the ranger station.

Tom was whistling happily, tucked behind the steering wheel of the Winnebago, Edmund silently seated next to him in the other captain's chair. I chose the kitchen bench to sit on because I could lean forward, resting my elbows on the table, cradling my head in my hands. Since I hadn't taken my shirt off in public for over twenty years, my sunburn was killing me, my back being especially tender. I just knew if I leaned back, the shirt I was wearing would feel like shards of broken glass on raw skin.

Soon I could look forward to blisters. When I was a youngster, these blisters used to pop on Sunday mornings in church. Then came the peeling and the contest with friends to see who could pry free the largest section of his skin. I once impressed a very sweet girl when I produced a peel as big as the flag in our fourth-grade classroom.

Sun poisoning can be pretty disgusting. Yet, it was a price I'd still be willing to pay for the admiration of a fine woman like... Jessica Quaggenblocker.

It was hard to believe we'd just met. I normally don't fall for a woman so quickly. I didn't know whether to chalk it up to God's gift of love at first sight or the fact that I hadn't had a date since the Nixon years.

The thought of Jessica reminded me that I was very angry at

Edmund. I was certain he had whispered something like, "Sorry about this, Jessica. I know you can do a lot better than Bill." Why would my best friend feel the need to sabotage this potential romance?

"We still haven't done any clamming," Tom commented to the windshield ahead of him. "Everybody clams while they're here. Why do you think they call this campground The Happy Clam?" Tom was rambling, almost incoherently. He didn't want Edmund and me to have a chance to get into another argument. "We haven't had any clam chowder yet, either," he continued. "These restaurants around here make the best clam chowder you'll ever taste!"

Edmund and I sat in obedient silence as Tom drove on.

"I brought a couple of kites with me that we can fly tomorrow on the beach. One of them is a one-stringer, the other has two strings—it's a tough little cookie to operate—takes both hands, but I'll bet between the three of us, we can handle it."

Tom's monologue was starting to sound like the drone of a vacuum.

"After all, we are a team, aren't we?"

Tom's question must have stumped us both— no answer was offered, and he pressed on. " I noticed some families playing badminton today while we were riding the Funcycles. I think tomorrow we should walk down there and challenge them to a match. I wouldn't be surprised if Meg packed a few racquets somewhere in our stuff. With the athletic ability in our group, we should be able to mop them up."

Edmund and I are as athletic as grout, so I didn't quite understand this comment until I realized that Tom was probably thinking of challenging them with Betsy, BJ, and Brandon as his foursome.

"We need to get a couple of nice photos of the three families together for our scrapbook," Tom said, moving on to the next item in his imaginary agenda. I wondered briefly if the Winnebago doors were locked from the inside. "We haven't taken many pictures at all. Plus we have the video camera we need to use as well."

Tom was right. Like typical Americans we'd brought hundreds of dollars' worth of cameras and video recorders, and now felt pressured to use them. Unfortunately, a guy can either use the equipment, or participate with his family and friends. "All right, you guys ride the Funcycles, while I video you speeding down the beach!" Or worse, "Okay, I'll just put down my fishing pole and film one of my best friends catching a huge fish, only to be violently thrown into the lake by one of my other best friends!"

"We also need to have another family-sing around the campfire. That was excellent." Tom continued working on us like a slow migraine, so that Edmund and I both sighed a collective sigh when we saw the sweet words: *Sewage Dump.*

Tom turned off the engine, and we all piled out to see what we could already smell. It was just a huge hole in the ground. The odor was, as we expected, distinctive. The faintest whiff of a disinfectant survived, but overall, its stronger-smelling enemy was winning.

"Edmund, give me a hand with the hose, will you?" Tom asked as they both went to fetch their prized possession from Pine Woods Hardware Store. Sure enough, a giant elephant's trunk, the camper's umbilical cord, appeared from the side of the Winnebago.

"I'll climb underneath to hook it up," Edmund offered.

I stood off to the side (my newfound place of greatest assistance) and watched as Edmund got down on the ground, belly up, and slid under the back of the motor home. *This must be a real rush for Edmund*, I decided. *Here is a guy whose entire life takes place at a desk behind an adding machine.*

"Do you see the outlet?" Tom asked.

"Yup. Here it is," he responded triumphantly.

"Well let me remind you to hook up the hose before you open the vents," Tom added, laughing.

Edmund laughed back, "Yeah, that might be a problem if I got my order of events mixed up. Whoa Nellie!"

I smiled at the mental picture of Edmund inadvertently opening the vent before he hooked up the hose. And I almost laughed out loud at the image of Edmund singing a Muddy Waters tune. *That'll teach you to mess with my girl!* I thought with fiendish glee.

Edmund knew what he was doing, however, and in a very short time the hose was lying deep in the public hole while we listened reverently to the tank emptying.

"Good work, Edmund," Tom said encouragingly. "It won't be too long, I'm guessing, before I see a motor home parked in the driveway outside the Holmeses' house."

"Yeah, that'd be nice." Edmund replied.

But I was nowhere near converting from my belief that camping vehicles were invented as extended punishment from God for wild, unrepentant sinning in an earlier stage of one's life.

I thought back to all the Saturday morning coffee I had shared with Edmund over the years. I recalled all the times he shared with me how much he would love to have a motor home, just like Tom's. I remembered when I used to be supportive, just like he used to be with me.

"I agree with Tom." I decided to put in my two cents. "I think you'd do well with a motor home, Edmund."

"Well, thanks, Bill," Edmund looked up from the drainage hole, a bit startled at a kind word proceeding from my mouth.

I couldn't resist one more little dig. "And I don't know much about operating camping equipment, but I do know this much:

you have found your calling. You really know how to empty the sewage!"

"THAT DOES IT! I WILL NOT STAND FOR ANYMORE OF THIS ABUSE!" Edmund was redder than I was, which is really quite red for any human being. If my eyes didn't deceive me, it looked like he was about to lift up the hose and aim it at me.

"Relax, friend," Tom was saying in soothing tones. Edmund put the hose back down the hole.

"NO. NO MORE 'RELAX.' THIS GUY HAS BEEN ON MY CASE FROM THE START AND I'M SICK OF IT!" Edmund was screaming so loudly that people who were waiting their turn to empty their tanks were starting to move along, thinking they would stop back later when the mentally imbalanced man had left for the day.

My own temperature was rising. "I think we need some clari-fication here, buddy-boy," I said. "You are the one who has been on my case from the beginning. I think you've got things turned around in your mind."

"We all just need to settle down and talk this through calmly," Tom kept repeating.

Then it happened. Edmund just blurted it out matter-of-factly, like it was something else to add to a grocery list, or a final score from the sports section. "Bill, I think it was a real mistake to invite you on this vacation."

The power of that statement rammed my solar plexus like a Civil War cannon ball at close range. I kept my balance, but my insides felt like they had fallen out all over the ground.

"Now, you don't mean that," Tom said, desperate to stitch up the gaping hole Edmund had just made.

"Yes, I do," Edmund replied quietly. The only other sound was the tank draining through the hose.

"Can you pull your tent trailer with your Lexus?" I suddenly blurted out.

"Yes," Edmund replied. "Why?"

"Because I'm gonna borrow your rental van, take my kids, and split. I'm outta here."

The weight of these words was enough to sink us into the sewage drain, but somehow we maintained our positions.

"Bill, Bill, Bill," Tom pleaded.

"No, Tom. Maybe Edmund's right. Maybe it was a mistake to come with you guys. Let's finish dumping these tanks and then I'll gather up my gang and head out."

"I think you'll be making a mistake," Tom exhorted. "The wise thing to do, the godly thing to do, the biblical thing to do is to sit down and talk this out as brothers. The passage in Matthew is clear concerning what to do when dealing with offenses...."

"Well, according to my 'brother,'" I interrupted mockingly, "I have already made my mistake by coming on this camping trip."

Edmund was silent, and I couldn't tell if he was shocked or if he'd gotten the response he wanted. I couldn't believe it...the guy who truly was my best friend now felt like my worst enemy. How could this have happened? What in the world had I done to be so offensive to this guy, who really was my brother, not only in our shared Christian faith, but in so many other emotional ways throughout all these years?

I didn't know exactly what to do, but I knew I had to get out of town.

I needed time to think. I needed time to sort things through. My kids were going to be angry beyond description. I might as well transport five portable volcanoes to their next sight for eruption. It would probably be so hot in the van, we'd melt the upholstery, the dashboard, and even the windows.

I knew I couldn't stay. I was in need of a sanctuary, a temple where I could feel the very presence of God as he communicated to me his understanding of this matter.

I won't go straight home, I concluded silently. *I know a place where I can go to commune with God, and at the same time keep my kids from being angry at me. Plus, being here at the Happy Clam, I'm halfway there already.*

And so, less than one hour later, the six of us piled in the rental van and headed down Highway 101 south to our destination of quiet sanctuary.

We were on our way to Dodger Stadium.

Chapter Ten

By the time we were nearing Los Angeles, night had already fallen. The kids, exhausted from their day on the beach, were all asleep in the back of the van. I glanced at them occasionally through my rearview mirror, noticing how pleasant they looked. I've always liked watching my kids sleep. They're so angelic, so unable to back-talk or complain.

Meg and Jenny had really cleaned them up nicely. This made me think of Jenny's thoughtful attempt to hook me up with Jessica Quaggenblocker, which sunk me into deeper despair. I couldn't believe I had waited this long for a blind date who had real appeal and then I had to meet her looking like a botched undersea experiment of Jacques Cousteau's.

Yes, the kids were all clean, asleep, and peaceful, but up front their driver was dirty, awake, and troubled.

Tomorrow night it would all come together at Dodger Stadium, I assured myself. We were too late for tonight's game. And I would never even consider going to catch the last few innings. That would be like showing up for the last fifteen minutes of church, or watching *Forrest Gump* only from Lieutenant

Dan and Vietnam on, neglecting the all-important childhood years before Gump turned into Tom Hanks.

Driving south, the lights of the city lit up the night sky. It was a relatively smog-free night and if you were absolutely silent, you could almost hear the theme to *L.A. Law* in the background. I was making a beeline for the city of Anaheim, specifically the Howard Johnson's on Harbor Boulevard, directly across the street from Disneyland. It had been our home away from home on many happier summer vacations in the past.

There's the problem right there! I thought as I waited at the red light on the corner of Harbor and Katella. *I should never have allowed myself to be talked into such a primitive vacation. Since when do I define relaxation as sleeping on the ground while smothering in a collapsed tent?*

I pulled into the hotel's parking lot, turned off the engine, told the kids to keep on sleeping and that I'd wake them up when I finished checking in. Once in the lobby, I was greeted by the night clerk, who was unbelievably perky for this hour of the night. He was young, about twenty-five, and he was wearing the company uniform of white shirt, maroon tie, and tan slacks.

"Good evening, my name is Paul. May I help you?" He said all this without looking up.

"Yes, I need a couple of rooms for the night."

"That's why we're here," he said, raising his head from his paperwork. At the sight of me Perky Paul gasped, his eyes widening as he took a step back from the counter.

Let's face it…I was a mess. Little had changed from earlier in the day, except that it all had time to ripen. I was still wearing the Cowboys T-shirt, and I put back on the red Hawaiian shirt once the sun went down. The real shocker had to be my head. My face was burned beet red, still splotched with Funcycle chain grease, and green residue from the bottom of Lake Gomez still clung to my face and hair.

I looked way too old for green spiked hair, which threw Perky Paul into a tailspin. He probably couldn't decide if I was:

—homeless
—a wayward biker
—a drug dealer
—or just a common middle-aged guy who was knee deep in his midlife crisis.

"Do you have a reservation with us tonight?" Paul asked, trying desperately to recover his professionalism.

"No, I'm afraid we don't," I admitted. "This kind of came up at the last minute."

"I see," Paul answered, a surge of power coursing through his veins.

"But we stay here a lot," I countered. "You can look us up on the file. You'll see we're very good customers."

"Can I see a major credit card?" he asked, seemingly convinced that I was living in a fantasy world. Not only had I never stayed there, he figured, I was probably too irresponsible to carry a credit card.

"I have VISA or American Express," I replied, fishing (the perfect term to use here) through my wallet. I handed him both cards, and once he brushed aside the green residue, he had to admit that I was official, though slimy.

"Since you don't have a reservation, the room will be a little more expensive," Paul explained, as he pushed a clipboard over my direction for my signature.

"How much is 'a little more'?" I asked.

"Oh, just a tad!" Perky gushed.

He ran my card through the scanner, and before I knew it two major goals were accomplished:

1) We had two rooms for the night.
2) I discovered that a "tad" equals forty dollars per night per room.

I pulled the van around to the spot closest to the door nearest to the room we were staying in. Since we were some of the last people to check in, certain hotel "laws" were in effect. We had to park so far away that we were actually under a sign saying Holiday Inn. Once inside Howard Johnson's, we had another five miles of hotel corridor to trek before arriving in front of our room. The kids all walked in front of me in an attempt to avoid the down-wind odor and gather enough speed to look like we weren't together.

"Where's the key, Dad?" the kids pestered, once we arrived at the right door.

I fumbled with my suitcases in an attempt to find the flimsy piece of plastic they now call a key. Finally I found the card stuck to the bottom of my suitcase. It took me several tries to make it work.

We had two adjoining rooms, a blessing and a curse. Part of me wanted to be a good father and lovingly care for my five little stair steps. The other part of me wanted a wall between me and the stair steps. I needed time alone to think. Children and thinking don't go together—never have, never will.

The kids were thirsty so I sent them down the hall to get cans of Coke from the vending machine we passed during our hike in. Each one wanted his/her own can, so I gave Betsy a ten-dollar bill, reminding her I expected change. She returned three minutes later, saying she needed another five.

Dejected, I handed her my soggy wallet and she scurried down the hall.

"We all got Cokes, Dad!" Bo announced as the five reentered the room.

"Was fifteen dollars enough?" I mocked.

"Brandon kicked in a few bucks, so we were covered," Betsy answered honestly. Hotels are geared to more creature comforts than tents, but they're a lot less comfortable for a wallet.

"I'm starved, Pops," BJ informed me, after plopping down on the bed next to mine.

"Me, too."

"Me three."

"Same here."

"Ditto."

The gang had spoken. I had to admit, I was a bit hungry myself. "Well, you know what?" I asked, a broad smile suddenly appearing on my kisser. "We're not camping anymore, so we don't have to limit our food choices to fish, moss, tree bark, or wienies."

"Do you mean… ?" the kids asked, collectively crossing their forty fingers and ten thumbs.

"I sure do!" I assured them.

"Hip, hip, hooray!" they shouted with glee. "We have the best dad in the whole world!"

"You've got that right," I kidded. "Now, I think we'd all feel better if I jumped into the shower before we ate. Am I reading all of you correctly on that count?"

"Amen!" Betsy exclaimed.

"Right on!" BJ sang.

"Preach it!" Brandon chimed in.

"Glory!" Ben shouted, pounding his fist on the dresser top.

"You stink, Daddy!" Bo added. The revival meeting metaphor had utterly escaped him.

"All right then. Let me take a quick shower and then we'll all go across the street to—"

"McDonald's!" my five finished my sentence.

I don't know when Quarter Pounders and Big Macs got confused with home-cooked meals at our house, but I'd be willing to wager it has its roots in my early days as the cook. After a week of burnt Hamburger Helper, macaroni and cheese so hard that it led to dental bills, and microwaved frozen lasagna, that red cardboard box of French fries can look like Chateaubriand.

I dragged myself into the bathroom where I closed the door, making doubly certain it was locked. I found the complimentary bath bar the size of a book of matches and hand soap the size of a book of matches ripped in half. They were placed on the back of the toilet, next to a microscopic container of shampoo/conditioner that would provide rich foamy lather for about three square inches of scalp. Why do hotels skimp on such necessities, yet go all out on shower caps and shoe-shine rags?

As I began to disrobe, I couldn't help but notice my lower body was as white as the Polar Ice Cap, my middle section was as red as Santa's coat, and my head was as green as lime sherbet.

Fortunately, I had my own toiletries bag with me, since I needed the jumbo family-size bottle of shampoo to launch a full frontal attack on the stiff green spikes that used to be my hair.

As I allowed the streams of life to caress my back, my mind unconsciously turned its attention to the debacle of the camping trip. Silently, I began ticking off the misadventures of the last few days:

—Made the unfortunate mistake of telling my kids about the camping invitation in the first place.

—Failed to grasp the "swing radius" principle, thus driving the Winnebago into that poor guy's old bucket of bolts.

—Lost the firewood contest, almost got arrested for attempting a chainsaw massacre, and suffered from secondary smoke inhalation during the campfire.

—Tried to sleep with a collapsed tent resting on our slumbering faces.

—Caught the biggest fish of the day. Got dunked. Lost the biggest fish of the day.

—Found the love of my life, only to lose her because I looked and smelled like Moby Dick.

—Spent grueling hours on the beach walking my Funcycle back to Freddie, who charged me extra for his inferior equipment.

—Strained lower back muscles, made hamburger of right hand, sunburned body, and suffered massive emotional injuries with potentially long-term effects.

"Why, God?" I asked suddenly, "Why did this trip get so totally screwed up?"

God, who speaks in various and sundry manners and times, chose to remain silent in my shower. Maybe he didn't have an answer. Maybe he was just trying to help me get to McDonald's.

What a treat to put on clean clothes! The kids were ready for me, each of them doing his or her impersonation of a human being starving to death. Throwing on my blue Dodger cap, I yelled, "Last one out of the room is a Giants fan!"

We zipped across the street to the Golden Arches. In true starvation form, we all ordered the Super Value Meals and we all

Super-sized them. As I paid with two more soggy twenty-dollar bills, I realized that I had spent more money in the last hour than I had in the last three days. But hey, that's what family vacations are all about, right? Quality time, quality food, quality accommodations, big bucks.

We found a booth in the back between the McDonald's Men's Room and the McDonald's Women's Room that gave us some privacy. We discussed our proposed schedule for tomorrow, which consisted of sleeping in (thunderous applause from all the teenagers), a late breakfast, an afternoon at the hotel's pool, and then back up the freeway for a 7:30 start between the Dodgers and the Phillies. Everyone agreed that tomorrow would be a most enjoyable day.

Then the six of us relived the last few days, taking turns telling stories and spreading laughter. Brandon had us all in stitches retelling the tent-pitching story. ("The family that pitches together ditches together!" he summarized.) Betsy disclosed how Charlotte and Patti really thought they should get their dad a Barbie doll as a gift next Christmas. BJ got out of the booth and dramatically retold the journeys we made on the bicycles. And Bo said he thought it was really cool that we slept in a tent that was so low to the ground.

I loved to hear my children reflect fondly on circumstances and events that we've had as a family.

Our conversation was rudely interrupted by the sound of explosions. "It's time for the fireworks at Disneyland!" my kids screamed in unison. We all sprinted outside to the parking lot. Since this McDonald's was directly across the street from the Magic Kingdom, we were treated to a fireworks extravaganza for free. The six of us stood between an old Ford pickup and a new Mercedes and looked to the sky.

"Maybe the camping trip wasn't so bad," I found myself think-ing more than once as we watched the many colors light up the sky. "We sure made some memories." And then, for the first time in months, a truly deep thought occurred to me: "If only we could have these kinds of pleasant memories without having to actually live them out first!"

Chapter Eleven

The drive to Dodger Stadium was a blend of excitement, anticipation, and boredom. The six of us were pumped about returning to Chavez Ravine, the gorgeous setting for one of the most beautiful ballparks in the country. That feeling helped pass the time while sitting absolutely motionless on the world's longest parking lot—Interstate 5 during rush hour.

There really isn't a rush hour in Los Angeles. More accurately, there are three hours in the entire day when the freeways aren't jammed. I simply didn't have the heart to put my kids on the road between 1:30 and 4:30 in the morning.

Like so many other Boomers, I grew up with a transistor radio in my ear. When the rest of the world was upside down and your mom was yelling at you and there were too many chores for one boy to handle and you didn't know which way to turn, you could count on baseball. Of course, baseball has had its share of scandal. But when you're a little boy, nothing is more pure, more heavenly, and more filled with hope than a major league baseball game.

When, on the rare occasion you could attend a game in person, baseball seemed to deliver almost as much spiritual effect as church, plus you could buy food and eat it right there in the pews.

Even as an adult, I have developed a pattern of making significant decisions during baseball games:

—I decided to become a speech teacher during the eighth inning of a Phillies-Pirates game back at the old Connie Mack Stadium in Philadelphia.

—I proposed to my soon-to-be wife during the seventh inning stretch of a Cardinals-Cubs game at Busch Stadium in St. Louis.

—I found out we were expecting our first child a year later during a Dodger-Padres game.

—Edmund took me to Candlestick Park a few years ago in order to break the news to me that I had lost a significant amount of money in an investment scheme that had gone sour. Appropriately, the Giants were playing the Reds.

Yes, the ballpark was a place of solace, a place for decisions, a place for contemplation of one's past, present, and future.

As my family trooped into the stadium, we looked like total fans, all six of us wearing some sort of Dodger paraphernalia. Even with the traffic, we were there at 6:05, exactly one hour and a half before the opening pitch. It looked to be a lovely night, weatherwise. The afternoon's heat had slowly given way to cooler evening air.

The lights were already on in the stadium. I took in a deep breath, and in doing so I whiffed the smells of Dodger dogs, popcorn, and some sort of cleaning fluid that they use in the public rest rooms.

It was the smell of fun.

As I had always done on my previous visits, I purchased my tickets through the front desk at Howard Johnson's. Even though it gave many people the appearance of a motel run by Mom and Pop, they were tied into the scalper pipeline, always able to get you tickets to everything from Disneyland to *Phantom of the Opera* to Jay Leno to the Dodger game. And they were good seats, too, no back-row Baptist kinds of choices.

Cranking through the turnstiles on the ground floor of the stadium, I observed that we were heading toward the third-base side, and judging by the row numbers, I estimated that we were about eight rows back, right behind the Dodger dugout on the left side of the field. Perfect!

Since we were there early, the teams were still in the clubhouse, going over last-minute strategy before ascending the dugout stairs for batting and fielding practice.

"I'm hungry, Dad!" Bo was first to announce his desire for food. Actually, all five kids were hungry, but in true family fashion, when I wasn't looking, they all put their youngest brother up to the task of hitting up the old man for food.

"All right, let's go get a dog and a Coke before BP," I answered nonchalantly.

"BP?" Ben echoed.

"Batting practice," Brandon explained. "I heard Uncle Tom use that abbreviation a few weeks ago. I just knew Dad would pick it up and try to act cool."

I winced. Brandon had nailed me .

We walked back to the snack bar under the long steel beams that held the stadium together. "Can you believe we're standing right over the Dodger clubhouse?" I asked the kids.

Their eyes widened. "Really?"

"Yep," I replied confidently, sharing another piece of information Tom had given me. "Right below us is their locker room."

"Wow!" Bo said, trancelike. Baseball is still a big thing when you're ten. Almost as big as it will be when you're forty.

"Six Dodger dogs, six large Cokes, two bags of popcorn, and four bags of peanuts," I said to the attendant, who looked as if she'd been working there since the move from Brooklyn.

"Fifty-four dollars," she barked back, never once looking up from her task of filling six Coke cups to a precise level.

"Ouch!" I replied, hoping for a little sympathy.

"Yer outta here!" she shot back, handing me our stuff. "Who's next up? Move it along."

We hiked back to our seats, settling in to watch batting practice, which had just begun for the Dodgers. The six of us were all engrossed in finding our favorite players. We found Mike Piazza, we found Brett Butler, we found Eric Karros, and we found Todd Worrell.

I saw new manager Bill Russell, and in typical old-man fashion, I flashed back to the days when Bill Russell was an infielder. My mind's eye conjured up Orel Hershiser, Fernando Valenzuela, and Kirk Gibson. Who could ever forget Gibson's ninth-inning home run against the Oakland As in the first game of the '88 World Series? It may just have been the finest moment in Dodger history. And there was Tommy Lasorda jumping up and down, running from the dugout to the field, as fast as his little bow-legs would carry him.

But as Piazza knocked two in a row into the left-field bleachers, my thoughts landed on Edmund again. *How could my best friend treat me so rotten? What was this all about?*

I was determined to not let my stress over Edmund get in the way of my enjoyment of the game. But everything reminded me of a good friendship gone bad. Finally, when our food was gone, the game was ready to start. We stood for the singing of the national anthem by John Cougar Mellancamp. I could hear Edmund leaning over to me in a whisper, saying "That's Francis Scott Key," and me thinking he was referring to the singer.

Hideo Nomo took the mound for the Dodgers and I could hear Edmund giving me precise figures on win/loss records, innings pitched, and earned-run averages up to the most current statistics available. He also knew salaries, contract status, as well as shoe and hat sizes. As much as I always griped about his incessant need to spout off statistics, without him nearby, I felt lost in a maze of undisclosed facts.

The evening's opponent was the Philadelphia Phillies, the team of my youth. And, just as in the days of my youth, they still had one of the worst records in the national league, and it was soon apparent why. The Dodgers were up 5-0 by the time the Phillies came to bat in the fourth inning. Piazza, a native Philadelphian, seemed to enjoy the game against his hometown team, and his two home runs in his first two at-bats were solid indication of his pleasure.

By the top of the sixth a lot of fans were starting to get bored due to the one-sided nature of the game. But I stared at every player, focused on every pitch, zeroed in on every play. On the outside it looked like I was the consummate baseball fan, but on the inside, I was so torn up over losing my best friend that I couldn't think of anything else. Something had to happen.

Right there, in the middle of Row H on the third base side of Dodger Stadium, I did something I can never remember doing in all my previous visits to the park.

I prayed.

"Dear Lord," I silently beseeched, "I know you probably want to watch the game, although with your omniscience and this commanding Dodger lead, I think we're safe here for a couple of minutes.

"I'm really upset about Edmund and me. I don't even know how it all got started, but I need your help. He's the best friend I've ever had and I miss his friendship big time. You know how hard it is for me to operate solo. I mean, I really believe you brought Edmund and Jenny into my life at just the right time.

"Eric Karros just hit a triple, Lord, but you already knew that.

"I miss Edmund's counsel, I miss his advice, I even miss his stats on all the major sports teams. This tension between the two of us is gonna eat me up. Lord, somehow, can you work it out so we can talk this through just as soon as we all get back home to Pine Woods?

"There's a pinch-hitter for Nomo, so he must be finished, as I'm sure you are aware.

"I don't know if you're going to need to perform a miracle or anything, but the sooner we can hash this out, the better.

"Thanks for helping me out here, Lord. Now, more than ever, I know I need you and I also need the friends you have given me in my life. Well, the inning is over, so I will sign off. Amen."

"It's time for the seventh-inning stretch, Dad!" Bo announced, standing alone. Poor guy, he always confuses the top of the seventh with the middle of the seventh.

"Not yet, buddy," I responded, placing my arm around his shoulder. "Three more outs, and then we stretch!"

"Look, Dad," Brandon pointed to the pitcher's mound. "Nomo's finished and Worrell is in as reliever." We all smiled, for we all like Todd Worrell. No sooner had we made that visual discovery then we heard the following announcement over the public address system:

"May I have your attention, please? Now pitching for the Los Angeles Dodgers, number thirty-eight, Todd Worrell!" The six of us looked at one another with that "I already knew that" look. But the second announcement was a surprise:

"May I have your attention, please? Would Mr. Bill Butterworth please report to the snack bar behind Section 9 immediately? Thank you very much."

"Dad, were you just introduced after Todd Worrell?" Ben asked incredulously.

"Are you gonna play for the Dodgers, Dad?" Bo asked, his eyes round as saucers.

"He wasn't introduced, he was paged," Betsy clarified.

"Why would you be paged here at Dodger Stadium?" BJ asked.

"Don't they just do that for doctors in emergency situations?" Brandon quizzed.

"This is very strange," was all I could say.

"Dad?" Betsy asked again.

"What, Betsy?" I replied.

"Aren't you going to go back to the snack bar to see what this is all about?"

"Oh…yeah. I guess that would be a good idea," I replied, the thought having not dawned on me until she said it. "I'll be right back," I said, standing up and slowly making my way past the twelve people that separated me from the aisle.

"Go get 'em, Dad!" BJ cheered. "Maybe they need you to suit up for the ninth inning!" By now, all the people in our section were starting to stare at me.

"You guys behave yourselves," I admonished.

"We sure will, Mr. Bill Butterworth!" BJ responded, making certain the entire section was aware of my identity.

I thought it would feel better to be famous, but I had this sick feeling inside my belly, and it couldn't be blamed on the Dodger dogs. As I walked up the aisle, I didn't know what to expect. Maybe it was a contest that I won. Maybe I was to be awarded season tickets! I smiled from Rows L to Q at that thought. At Row R, I suddenly scowled, thinking it might be a representative from some collection agency, here to inform me my credit card payments are overdue. By Row X, I was back to a look of utter confusion.

So my heart skipped three or four beats when I saw a tall figure standing in front of the mustard, eating a Dodger dog.

"TOM!" I screamed from about twenty-five feet away.

"Hi, Bill!" Tom smiled, waving like we had just run into one another at the gas station.

"What are you doing here?" I asked.

"Bill, we need to talk," Tom replied with a serious look.

"We do?"

"Yes, we most certainly do."

"How did you know I was here?" I suddenly blurted out.

"When you left in such a huff yesterday, we figured you wouldn't be able to talk your kids into going straight home. So, the logical destination would be down here. Plus, you always stay at that Howard Johnson's across from Disneyland. We called them, and they confirmed that you were a guest of theirs, and that they had sold you six tickets to tonight's Dodger game. It was that simple."

"You're amazing," I said softly, impressed that Tom would go to all that effort to hunt me down, even though it was only a single telephone call.

"Not me, Bill. This was all accomplished by your buddy, Edmund."

"Edmund?"

"I want you to follow me," Tom instructed.

"Where are we going?"

"You ever been downstairs inside the clubhouse?"

"No. Is that where we're going? Are you taking me to the locker room?" I was pounding Tom with questions like a four-year-old.

"Yep. That's where we're going."

"Can we do this?" I asked.

"Sure. I still have lots of friends here at the stadium. They're allowing us to go downstairs so we can talk."

The part about talking didn't register, as I was beside myself with the anticipation of going down into the Dodger Stadium belly. We met up with a security guard, inconspicuously dressed in a bright orange blazer with matching hat. "Hello, Mr. Graham!" he smiled. "Come right through this door! You remember the way, don't you?"

Tom nodded, patted the guard on the back, and we were soon walking down a stairway that led us to a tunnel. "This way," Tom said, pointing to the right. "If you go left, you end up in the dugout!" I couldn't believe I was in the tunnel that led to the Dodger dugout! This was amazing.

We walked about five more yards to the right, and then Tom opened a door. As soon as I peeked in, I knew where I was. It was the locker room. Assorted street clothes were strewn all over the open lockers.

"Keep following me and please don't touch anything," Tom implored, as if he knew the incredible temptation I was experiencing as I saw all kinds of bats, gloves, baseballs, and caps.

"Where are we going?" I kept asking.

"I thought we'd sit down back in the manager's office. We can talk there."

"The manager's office?" I swallowed hard as I asked.

"That's right."

"You mean, Bill Russell's office?" I asked one more time for complete confirmation.

"Yes, although I still have a hard time thinking of it as his office," Tom admitted. "To me, it will always be Tommy Lasorda's. Did you know Tommy used to have a little stove in there? He was always cooking up some sort of pasta and sauce that would fill the entire clubhouse with the smell of an Italian restaurant."

I didn't know that and was about to say so. But before I could even get the words out, I walked into the office and felt my body jolt, just like it had been hit by lightning.

There, behind the desk, someone was sitting quietly. Not Bill Russell. And not Tommy Lasorda.

It was Edmund.

Chapter Twelve

Hello, Bill," Edmund said as calmly as Bogart in an old movie. I looked upward to the heavens, silently thanking God for miraculously answering my prayer. I wanted to hop over the desk and give Edmund a big old bear hug.

But in true manly form, I simply said, "Hello, Edmund." My voice was every bit as cool as his, turning our interpersonal chess game into a tie match.

"Like I said, I think it would be a good idea if we had a talk," Tom said, resuming his position as our referee.

I wanted to spill my guts, to apologize for whatever sin I had committed, to ask for forgiveness, to right whatever wrong I may have done. I just wanted things back on track with my best friend.

"Edmund, do you have something you want to say to Bill?" Tom asked.

"No, I'll let him go first," Edmund replied, completing an utter breach of apology etiquette.

"All right. Bill, do you have something you would like to say to Edmund?"

Sure I did, but his unwillingness to speak was bothersome. I was just about ready to pass the ball back to him, when the memory of my sixth-inning prayer pierced my gut. I had clocked out of a complete inning of Dodger baseball to ask God to make things right. Now, he had miraculously brought my friend into the very bowels of Dodger Stadium, and I was flirting with the audacity to zip my lip.

"I'm sorry, Edmund," I blurted out in such haste that it sounded more like "IzorryEhmon."

"Did you say you were sorry?" Tom asked.

"Yes," I said, taking a deep breath to regain some calm. "I am truly sorry, Edmund."

"Well, that's a good place to start," Tom encouraged, gazing back and forth between us.

"You don't even know what you're sorry for, do you, Bill?" Edmund stared as he spoke.

I hung my head. "No. I guess I have to be honest with you. I don't have any idea what this is all about."

"Well, let me tell you what it's all about," Edmund answered. "Do you remember the morning I called you to invite you to the hardware store to meet Tom and me to discuss the camping trip?"

"Kinda," I responded vaguely.

"That morning on the phone you said some things that I know you have felt for a long time. It was so hard for me to hear you actually say them. You really hurt me..." his voice trailed off.

"What did you say, Bill?" Tom prodded.

"I don't exactly remember," I confessed, feeling worse by the minute. I was sinking lower than the desk, heading for the floor. You could have used me to mop up any pasta residue that Lasorda may have left.

"You said, 'You CPAs are all alike.' 'You think all we need is the facts and then we crank out the numbers and everything will work out just fine.' Do you remember saying that to me, Bill?"

I decided to come clean. "I guess I sort of recall it—possibly."

Edmund seemed unmoved by my confession. "Well, it cut me to the quick, buddy," he went on. "Here I am, your best friend, and you blow me off on the phone, saying I fit some ridiculous stereotype that you've bought into about accountants. For your information, I don't think everything works out nicely just by crunching the numbers. You reduced me to some idiot and it's been gnawing at me ever since you said it."

Finally, I felt truly stunned. "I'm sorry, man," I whispered.

"Then Tom and I go to all this extra trouble to get you and your kids on this camping trip and you act like we're taking you to prison. You can be so ungrateful."

"Now hold on just a minute," I argued, regaining a little of my strength. "I told you from the start that camping wasn't my thing. I didn't want to go, but I felt I had no other option but to agree."

"Oh, are you still whining about that camping trip years ago with the bear and rescue squad and the jaws of life?" Edmund asked.

"It was very traumatic," I replied.

"Well, you know, I've talked with your claustrophobic friend, Fred, about that trip."

I swallowed hard. "You did?"

"Yes, I did," he answered. "And according to Fred, the story is a little different. He says it wasn't a bear, it was a raccoon. And he says that he wasn't the one who freaked out. He says it was you."

The silence was thick in the air.

"You've known all the time it was me?" I whispered hoarsely.

"Yes."

"Then why did you invite me on this camp out?"

"Exactly *because* I knew the whole story, buddy. It's like getting thrown from a horse—the best thing is to get right back on one. I honestly believed if I could get you and your kids out under the stars that you would have a whole new feeling toward camping."

"I see," I said, the full impact of Edmund's sincere concern sinking in.

"I was just trying to help, Bill…just like I was just trying to help with you and Jessica Quaggenblocker."

I paused a moment while Edmund's last statement sunk into my skull. "What did you say about Jessica Quaggenblocker?" I asked quietly.

"Jenny and I are very fond of Jessica, and we are very fond of you, too. We thought you would really hit it off, which would have made us very happy."

Edmund's kind words were causing me to blush. Embarrassed, I looked down at the desk. My eyes fell on Russell's notes on the Phillies (one line said, "Don't forget to ask Reuben Amaro to send me a bunch of Tastykakes when he gets back home.").

Edmund was continuing, "Jessica is exactly what you've told me you always wanted in a woman. And Jenny and I both felt that you would be a good match for her. I don't mean to sound super-spiritual about all this, but we actually prayed about the two of you for a long time before we decided to set something up. It just seemed so right."

His story was interrupted by a huge rumble above our heads, as if the ceiling were going to collapse. "Somebody just hit a home run," Tom explained. "And it wasn't one of the Phillies." We all smiled. Just thinking of a Dodger trotting the bases brought warmth to our souls. "Anyway, go on with your story, Edmund."

"When the three of us returned from our fishing fiasco and I realized that Jessica was going to be there to meet us, my heart sank. I really wanted her to have a positive first impression of you, and you can imagine what she must have thought when you showed up all covered with algae."

"Just a minute here," I interrupted. "As I recall the story, I distinctly remember it being *your* fault I was the Creature From the Green Lagoon, *and* I saw you whispering a little secret to Jessica."

"That's right, I did," Edmund confessed.

"It sure looked to me like you were putting me down."

"What in the world made you think that?"

"Whatever it was that you were saying to her, I can remember her looking back over her shoulder at me, smiling and sorta laughing."

"So you thought I was making fun of you?"

"Weren't you?"

"No, not at all!" he exclaimed, leaning toward me over the manager's desk. "Actually it was just the opposite."

"The opposite?"

"Yes. When I was whispering into Jessica's ear, I said, 'Jessica, I know he looks a little strange right now, but you really need to give this guy a chance. He's a great guy, the best friend I have ever had.'"

I couldn't believe my ears. So much of what I had been angry at Edmund about was an utter misunderstanding. "So when Jessica was looking my way and smiling, she really was smiling?" I asked.

"That's right, Bill," Edmund replied. "She is very interested in you."

"Wow!" I exclaimed, a faint glimmer of hope returning to my world. "I guess the camping trip wasn't a total disaster after all."

"Camping really is a great thing," Tom spoke up. "But I think I am learning that it's not for everybody."

"That's right," I added. "My kids love Disneyland. They love the Dodger game. They love a hotel. There's nothing wrong with that, as long as I can keep figuring out a way to afford it. There's nothing inherently wrong with a family who doesn't like to camp. We can still be a family, even a good Christian family."

"You're right, Bill," Edmund said again. "I am truly sorry that I gave you such a hard time about not being much into camping and all that goes with it."

"Well, I'm sorry too, man. This camping trip did teach me something. My life would be missing a lot if I didn't have you as my buddy. I can't believe how insensitive I was to your feelings. Guys like me who kid around a lot don't always realize that they can cross the line to genuine offensive behavior. You're not some stereotypical, number-crunching CPA. And, Lord knows you're not a 'everything always works out nicely' kind of guy. You wouldn't still be my friend if that was your motto, now would you?"

He looked up and laughed.

Then we both got to our feet. "Let's try to keep the communication lines open a little better in the future, okay?" I asked him as I extended my right hand for a handshake.

"Okay," my best friend replied, grabbing my arm, and pulling me over for a big-guy bear hug.

"I guess we should head on back up to see the end of the game," Tom suggested.

"That's a good idea, Tom," Edmund exclaimed. "I think Bill will be especially pleased to know that there's someone else who accompanied us to the game from our campsite."

"Did you bring Jenny?" I smiled.

He shook his head.

"Is Meg with you?"

"Nope."

"Well then, who's here?" I asked.

"A Miss Jessica Quaggenblocker," he replied, smiling a smile as big as a Winnebagel.

"Really?"

"Really. She wanted to see you again and I had high hopes that we could patch up our differences, so I invited her along."

"Thanks, Edmund, you're a real pal."

"Oh, it was nothing," he replied modestly. "She kinda likes you, but she *loves* the Dodgers!"

❖

Later, when Edmund and I would finally add up the score of the Great Big Fight, we decided we'd both learned a lot. I don't kid about areas in which he is sensitive anymore. Actually, I'm trying real hard to let him know how good an accountant I really think he is.

With all the things we have in common, Edmund and I are learning, sorta like any good married couple, to appreciate and respect our differences. He still camps and fishes. I still don't.

We also made a pact to get things off our chests before they brew into an explosion next time.

❖

The three of us walked through the tunnel of Dodger Stadium, enjoying the warmth of being reunited in our friendship. Tom had sent a note back up to one of the security guards, who had escorted my five kids and Jessica down to the tunnel. The kids were in a state of shock as they saw their Dad walk out of the clubhouse with Tom and Edmund. Their faces revealed joy, however, as they

149

could tell everything was back to normal just by looking at our smiles.

As if the sight of us three wasn't amazing enough, at that precise moment the game ended, filling the tunnel with a sea of men in white uniforms with blue hats.

"Tom Graham!" came a loud voice from down the tunnel.

"Todd Worrell!" Tom responded happily. "You pitched a great game out there tonight!"

"Thanks. That means a lot coming from a guy like you."

"Todd, I want you to meet some people. This is Bill Butterworth and his children, Betsy, BJ, Brandon, Ben, and Bo. And this is Jessica Quaggenblocker"

"Nice to meet you," Todd said politely, shaking each of our hands.

"You forgot someone, Tom," I added. "Todd, this is my best friend, Edmund Holmes."

Edmund shook Todd's hand, but looked gratefully at me.

"Well, it's nice to meet all of you," Todd said one more time. "I've got to go hit the showers." He walked to the clubhouse door, stopped before opening it, turned back toward us, and said, "Here's the baseball I just pitched to win the game. Bill, why don't you take it on behalf of all your family and friends?"

And with that, he tossed the ball in the air right in my direction. It was a great ending to a great adventure: Butterworth Takes the Baseball, and Decides to Keep It.

ATTENTION
BUTTERWORTH VACATION SURVIVORS!

If you enjoyed *Butterworth Takes A Vacation*—
you will love his first comedy novel:
Butterworth Gets His Life Together

Available at your local Christian bookstore.